JOHN WEBSTER

# The Duchess of Malfi

Orient BlackSwan Drama Classics

JOHN WEBSTER

# The Duchess of Malfi


*Editor*

Kajal Sengupta

*Formerly Reader in English, Presidency College, Kolkata*

*General Editor*

S. Viswanathan

*Formerly Professor of English University of Hyderabad*



Orient BlackSwan

**ORIENT BLACKSWAN PRIVATE LIMITED**

*Registered Office*
3-6-752 Himayatnagar, Hyderabad 500 029 (T.S), India
email: centraloffice@orientblackswan.com

*Other Offices*
Bangalore / Bhopal / Bhubaneshwar / Chennai
Ernakulam / Guwahati / Hyderabad / Jaipur / Kolkata
Lucknow / Mumbai / New Delhi / Patna


First published 2004
Reprinted 2015

ISBN 978 81 250 2621 1

*Typeset by*
OSDATA, Hyderabad 500 029

*Printed in India at*
Orion Printers
Hyderabad 500 004

*Published by*
Orient Blackswan Private Limited
3-6-752 Himayatnagar
Hyderabad 500 029
email: hyderabad@orientblackswan.com

# Contents

## Contents

# List of abbreviations used in the book

| | | |
|---|---|---|
| *WD* | : | *White Devil* |
| *M of V* | : | *Merchant of Venice* |
| *TN* | : | *Twelfth Night* |
| *Rom. and Jul.* | : | *Romeo and Juliet* |

# General Introduction

## Elizabethan and Jacobean Drama

Queen Elizabeth died in 1603 and in the same year was succeeded by James VI of Scotland who now became James I of England. It is these two monarchs who have given their name to English literature from the second half of the sixteenth century to the beginning of the seventeenth century—Elizabethan and Jacobean (from Jacobus, the Latin for James). This period saw the greatest flourishing of literature that England has ever known, in prose, in poetry, above all in drama. It is in this period that Shakespeare wrote his plays for he belongs to both ages. *Hamlet* was written around 1603 and all Shakespeare's tragedies and the last romances chronologically belong to the Jacobean period. Because of the extraordinary literary output of these years that span the reigns of both Elizabeth and James, critics often regard the literature of the early seventeenth century as a continuation of the previous age and they sometimes refer to the whole period as Elizabethan. The critical anthology edited by Ralph Kaufman which starts with essays on Lyly and goes on up to Massinger and Ford is entitled *Elizabethan Drama: Modern Essays in Criticism* and Rupert Brooke's book on Webster has the title *John Webster and Elizabethan Drama.*

Yet there is a difference. Una Ellis-Fermor, in her book *Jacobean Drama* distinguishes between the two ages. But she is over-simplistic with her compartmentalising of the kinds of plays written during this period and F. P. Wilson's compact book *Elizabethan and Jacobean* makes qualifications to the sharp changes emphasised by her.

The fact remains however, that though dramatic activity continued with the same ardour and momentum, a change was seen in the tone, the texture, even in practical matters like stagecraft and, above all, in the philosophical vision of plays written during the later period. But we must be careful of mere chronology. All Shakespeare's tragedies were written during the seventeenth century; yet there is a world of difference between the

Shakespearean tragic vision of life and that of Webster. In Shakespearean tragedies, though the pain and sufferings of Lear, Hamlet, Othello and Macbeth move us profoundly, there is, at the end, some sort of peace, some acceptance, if not understanding, of the incomprehensible world we live in. In Webster's *Duchess of Malfi* and *The White Devil* also, a conviction emerges that man can endure and survive, which in itself is an assertion of the triumph of man's unconquerable mind, but there is also a feeling that, like Kurtz, in Conrad's novel, we have entered the very heart of darkness, and like Kurtz, we also exclaim, 'The horror! The horror!'

The darkening of the world vision in drama cannot merely be interpreted as an increase in murder and blood-and-thunder scenes. There are many murders, much hatred, violence and blood revenge in the earlier plays and in the last scene of *Hamlet* four corpses lie on the stage. But in Webster there is also an element of morbidity, a psychological, almost sadistic gloating over suffering and a fascination for the horrors of death. The change is visible everywhere, not only in drama. Sir Thomas Browne broods over urn burials and muses on the different ways that people dispose of their dead, and Donne is fascinated by a bracelet of bright hair over a bone.

Why does this change come about? Why does Donne say in *The Anatomy of the World* that he sees all around him death, decay and corruption? Before proceeding to Webster it would be as well to study the times in which he lived and the forces that shaped the temper of his age.

## The Philosophical Background

The entire period that we have been discussing may be comprehensibly described as the period of the Renaissance. The mood may have changed in the Jacobean age but it is still the impact of the Renaissance that provides the literary impulse behind it and perhaps the best way to begin is to begin with the Renaissance.

The Renaissance had brought about the liberation of the human mind which, freed from the shackles of medieval Christianity, found delight in discovering itself. The Church had stressed upon spiritual values—*contemptus mundi, amor dei.* Reject this world and contemplate only God. The Church, through its vast hierarchy of priests, had the sole monopoly to instruct and teach and the individual had to follow the dictates of the Church without question. Of course, many cracks had appeared and long before the Renaissance there were schisms and signs of disintegration in the Church's totalitarian control of society. But whatever dissension there was, was beneath the surface, and even if the foundations were shaking, the structure and the fabric of the Church remained.

The discovery of the human mind and the awakening of the rational faculty and the conviction that man had a right to think for himself brought with it the birth of science. Instead of contemplating God, man began to study the physical universe; instead of shunning temporal existence he began to delight in the world around him and particularly in himself. Thus humanism was born and as early as the fourteenth century, Chaucer explores the infinite variety of human nature.

The immediate reaction, on one level, was an uncritical euphoric feeling of excitement over man's infinite potentialities and man's aspiration to acquire everything in the here and now of existence. Bacon claims that he has taken all knowledge for his province, Marlowe's Tamburlaine exclaims that a god is not so glorious as a king and Dr Faustus bids Divinity adieu.

But every time the exultation had to stop short in front of the grim and inescapable figure of Death which no man can ignore. Hand in hand with delight went the terrifying thought that Death ends all.

Death has always held a pivotal position in man's thoughts because it is the ultimate mystery, beyond which all is unknown. The attitude to death has changed from age to age and from this attitude often the spirit of the times can be perceived, but Time and Death have never surrendered their central position in human existence.

In the Middle Ages, writers were fascinated by death and much of medieval literature broods over it. *Everyman* describes the moment of death as do most of the morality plays and the *Pearl* poet grieves over the death of his little two-year-old daughter. The plague which ravaged Europe at this time brought the reality of death close to every home and the religious art of the thirteenth and fourteenth centuries played with macabre figures of skeletons and the Dance of Death. All this confirmed the belief that

> al nis but a fayr
> This world that passeth sone as floures faire
> (Chaucer, *Troilus and Criseyde*, Bk V)

and made man turn more resolutely to the religious assurance that beyond death, the soul entered the eternal bliss of heaven.

With the Renaissance all this was changed. The liberation of the human mind and the exploration of the material universe made this life suddenly more precious, more meaningful, far more exciting than vague assurances of an after-life which may just as well be, after all, deserts of vast eternity. Humanism had brought with it a reversal in the value system. The new age turned its gaze from heaven to earth, from implicit faith in the supernatural to rational analysis of empirical faith, from worship of God to glorification of man. In so doing, they found a new earth but they 'unsettled' the heavens.

At the back of the mind however, lay Time's winged chariot and the sinister unconquerable figure of Death. There were some who deliberately shut this thought from their minds and abandoned themselves to the enjoyment of the present moment for itself. 'Gather ye rosebuds while ye may' because 'what's to come is still unsure'. This *carpe diem* attitude to life however, was essentially escapist by nature and could satisfy only a few. For more serious thinkers it was necessary to search for permanence within the humanistic scale of values. And to some extent, they found this. Humanism brought its own form of idealism, not the Divine ideal, but human idealism. If we can perpetuate the ideal even at the cost of death, we perpetuate ourselves. The cause is above the individual, and death cannot destroy the cause.

> It is the cause, my soul, it is the cause,
> Let me not name it to you, you chaste stars,
> It is the cause.

Thus we see that the attitude of resignation that typified the medieval mind was replaced in the early Renaissance by a resistance, a defiance, and a determination not to surrender to death. Shakespeare in his sonnets, seeks ways and means to defeat 'this bloody tyrant Time'.

This state of mind however, could not last long for man cannot survive by ideals alone. He must live with life and this reality kept impinging on his mind. As emotion exhausted itself and the wave of patriotic excitement passed away, one eventual psychological reaction was the aftermath of euphoria, a reaction of, not depression, but a hang-over feeling after the jubilation of the night before. It must also be remembered that the initial excitement centred more upon the glorification of man than a sober assessment of his capabilities. The Renaissance was the 'rebirth' of the human mind which lay in the discovery of his faculty of reason and the birth of reason as already mentioned, meant the birth of science. Reason began to assert itself over emotion, and by the mid-seventeenth century, science and reason took control. The Royal Society for Improving Natural Knowledge was given the Royal Charter in 1662 and Hobbes, in his *Leviathan*, forbids men to use 'obscure, confused and ambiguous Expressions, also all metaphorical Speeches, tending to the stirring up of Passions.'

But before the stability of reason could establish itself, man found himself adrift in a sea of uncertainties. The knowledge gained from science and the cosmological impact of the new astronomy upset all preconceived beliefs. The medieval world picture which still persisted in the minds of many, even in the Jacobean age, was geocentric, hierarchical and immutable. Copernicus's world picture contradicted Christian dogma, Biblical authority and the immediate evidence of the senses and the old religious security which had given coherence and meaning to the universe could no longer satisfy. The Great Chain of Being which had imposed pattern and harmony to all existence, wherein all creatures had their allotted space, was disturbed. Man, by asserting his own supremacy, had broken the pattern, the string had been untuned, and discord followed. Life was no longer simple, the nature of man became complex, and bitter at its own complexity, while exultation was undercut by doubt. To try to arrive at the truth it was necessary to look at the worst and truth, or what appeared to be truth, brought with it morbidity, scepticism and despair. That way, madness lies. The recurring theme of madness in so many plays begins as early as Kyd's *Spanish Tragedy* where Horatio's death drives his mother mad and Hieronymo pretends to go mad to find out who the villain is. Hamlet is mad 'north-north west'. Ophelia loses her sanity, Lear rushes out in the night crying, 'O fool, I shall go mad' and in the heath, raves in fury. Lady Macbeth walks sleeplessly all night constantly washing her hands to get the smell of the blood off. The theme of madness recurs in Middleton and Rowley's *The Changeling* and it reaches its climax in *The Duchess of Malfi* with the choric symphony of madmen and the Duchess herself, tottering on the edge of sanity, ' I am not mad yet...yet I am not mad' (IV.ii. 24–6). In the end, the most horrible kind of madness, 'a very pestilential disease', lycanthropia, overcomes Ferdinand as he howls around churchyards, digging up bones, imagining, in a state of total dementia, that he is a wolf.

It seemed to many that the world was decaying in its old age, the last stage of a steady process of degeneration that had begun with the Fall of Man. 'The world's whole frame,' says Donne, 'is quite out of joint' in *An Anatomy of the World:* 'It is a sick world, yea dead, yea putrified'. Perhaps the most powerful comment on the state of confusion and bewilderment of man is given by Donne in his *First Anniversary* or *The Anatomy of the World.* It is worth quoting the whole passage:

> And new Philosophy calls all in doubt,
> The element of fire is quite put out.
> The Sunne is lost, and th' earth and no man's wit
> Can well direct him where to look for it
> And freely men confess that this world's spent
> When in the planets, and the firmament
> They seek so many new: they see that this
> Is crumbled out again t'his Atomies.
> 'Tis all in pieces, all coherence gone;
> All just supply, and all Relation,
> Prince, Subject, Father, Sonne, are things forgot.
> For every man alone thinks he hath got
> To be a Phoenix, and that there can be
> None of that kind, of which he is, but he.

*The First Anniversary* was published in 1611. In 1612 came *The White Devil* and Webster started working on *The Duchess of Malfi* shortly after. The gloom that prevails in Webster's two plays, and in much of Jacobean literature can therefore be largely explained by the intellectual climate of the age. The overhanging presence of Death from which none could escape, either through Divine idealism or human idealism, led understandably into an extraordinary blend of fascination and horror which deepened into a morbid preoccupation with Death. We see this in *Hamlet* as Hamlet holds Yorick's skull in his hands and muses. Many years later, T.S. Eliot, in *Whispers of Immortality,* writes of Webster and Donne:

> Webster was much possessed by death.
> And saw the skull beneath the skin
> And breathless creatures underground
> Leaned backwards with a lipless grin.
> Donne, I suppose was such another
> He knew the anguish of the marrow
> The ague of the skeleton.

To say this, however, is not to say all, and we cannot conclude on the basis of this alone that Webster holds a negative nihilistic view of the universe. It is necessary to go a little deeper into his age and into his plays, if we wish to understand his interpretation of life.

## The Social and Economic Background

There were several other factors that led to the troubled mental state of this period of history and on the immediate level problems arose that endangered the security of day-to-day existence. To begin with, there was uncertainty over the succession. After Elizabeth who? With the accession of James this was solved but the state of uncertainty once roused, takes time to settle down, and in the meantime, the Jesuits went on a rampage. Elizabeth had issued a proclamation in 1602, banishing the Jesuits, and events abroad—the defeat of the Spanish Armada, the recognition of England as a supreme naval power and the increase of wealth through the East India Company's trading activities—had pandered to national and patriotic pride and distracted the public mind. But now attention turned to matters at home and religious factionalism which had been imperfectly suppressed, rose to the surface. In quick succession, three Catholic plots to overthrow James were discovered and suppressed, the most well-known of them being the Gunpowder Plot of 1605.

This added to the general air of uncertainty but certain other fundamental changes were taking place which were beginning to turn the very fabric of society upside down. The feudal structure of society had come into being after the Norman Conquest. The barons who owned almost the whole of the countryside had total control over the rural community and they exerted their power and authority to such an extent that the king became almost a puppet in the hands of the barons who, often warring with each other, in effect, controlled England. Eventually, after Henry Richmond killed Richard III at Bosworth and became Henry VIII, a powerful monarchy came into being and the feudal system collapsed. Politically, the end of feudalism marks the end of the Middle Ages. But on the socioeconomic level the community continued with feudal customs and the feudal ways of life. Wealth still belonged to the aristocracy and they went on living in their grand style with their courts and huge bodies of retainers and exercising their powers of patronage. And further, being now divested of all responsibilities, they became increasingly dissolute in their way of life.

But a new force was emerging and another section of the community which had originated with the medieval trade guilds was beginning to acquire wealth and could not be ignored. The end of feudalism marks also the birth of capitalism, and by the middle of the seventeenth century, the society was in a state of transformation. The fundamental changes involved in moving from a corporate feudal order, however degenerate, to the greater individualism of the capitalistic system, had started much earlier. What we see now is a period of accelerated change. The urban middle class consisting of merchants, bankers, entrepreneurs, flourished and proportionately, landowners and the masses, both urban and rural, suffered. The drift of nobility to towns and the steady purchase of estates by the wealthy citizens led to the breakdown of traditional values. The new rich, while assuming economic control, did not know or did not care about the old courtly pattern of society. They were unwilling to continue with the feudal and paternalistic codes of behaviour and this led to a decline in the traditional activities of the nobility and the gentry, like hospitality, charity and patronage.

Yet the glamour and the glitter of the court remained. Only, it became increasingly corrupt, with sexual and political intrigue adding to the complexity. The motif of political corruption and moral and sexual degradation centred in a court is a recurring theme in the plays of Marston, Webster and Tourneur. But it was distanced in time and place and presented in a framework other than that of England. A natural transference was to the Italian setting and the notorious world of Florence and the de Medicis. (One of the characters in *The White Devil* is Francisco de Medici, Duke of Florence). The Jacobeans may not have read the works of the Italian historian Francisco Guicciardini (1483–1540) who wrote an account of Florence that is full of cynical realism, but the corruption and immorality of Italian courts was well-known. Stories of intrigue, of plotting, of sex and murder, particularly of poisoning—an exotic art involving scientific knowledge—fascinated the dramatists of the period. In *The White Devil*, Isabella, the wife of Brachiano, kisses his poisoned painting and dies, and in The *Duchess of Malfi* the Cardinal makes Julia kill the poisoned pages of the Bible and she dies.

The movement of people from country to town has swelled the urban population while, at the same time, during Elizabeth's reign many new grammar schools had been founded. This resulted in a steady rise of educational activity and a consequent increase of educational aspirations. In 1611, Bacon wrote to the king:

> .....for grammar schools there are already too many...there being more scholars than the state can prefer and employ.... it must need fall out that many persons will be bred unfit for other vocations and unprofitable for that in which they were bred up, which fill the realm full of indigent, idle and wanton people.

We see now the emergence of a phenomenon that one is familiar with in India—a rise in the number of educated unemployed. The dangers of over-education, unemployment and thwarted ambitions are obvious. These men were not organised as they are today into unions and each had to fend for himself. Sycophancy increased and to obtain a job or a placement in court they were prepared to carry out all kinds of orders, however degrading, however unethical. Prototypes of this section of the community are Flamineo in *The White Devil* and Bosola in *The Duchess of Malfi.* Flamineo complains to his mother:

> You brought me up
> At Padua, I confess, where, I protest
> I have been fain to heel my tutor's stockings,
> At least seven years; conspiring with a beard
> Made me a graduate; then to the duke's service
> I visited the court, whence I returned,
> More courteous by far, more lecherous by far,
> But not a suit the richer.
>
> (*W D*, I.ii.339–48)

Dissatisfaction breeds cynicism, makes people surly and begets melancholy. The cynical man finds a relief in railing against the world and often uses his wit as a kind of defensive–offensive with which to assure himself of his own superiority. The emergence of the Malcontent in Jacobean drama becomes almost inevitable. We have an early example of Monsieur Melancholy in Jacques in Shakespeare's *As You Like It* and a more acerbic cynic in Thersites in *Troilus and Cressida,* Marston's play has the title character *The Malcontent*, who is Giovanni Alto Fonte, deposed king of Genoa, disguised as Malvole. In *The Revenger's Tragedy,* Vindice speaks of discontent, the noble man's consumption and Antonio in *The Duchess of Malfi* refers to this 'foul melancholy' of Bosola.

The melancholy humour was not of course, a creation of Jacobean drama. Interest in men led to the study of human nature and of the psychology of behaviour. Numerous books of 'characters' appeared throughout the seventeenth century. Hall's *Characters of Virtues and Vices* published in 1608 was followed by Overbury's *Characters* and many others in the same vein. Casaubon's edition of Theophastus had been published as early as 1592. Analysis of character types developed into a literary genre that was further encouraged by Jonson and his Humours. The melancholy man became a favourite type to study and both genuine and affected melancholy appear regularly in literature.

It is also worth noting that woman is now emerging as an entity that does not fit into the traditional patriotic concepts of a patriarchical society where she was held under total subjugation. Queen Elizabeth herself led the way, dominating and controlling England for forty-five years. As early as the fifteenth century the *Paston Letters* indicate that in an ordinary well-to-do middle class household women conducted business affairs with an efficiency and authority equal to that of their husbands. In literature the first feminist is possibly Chaucer's Wife of Bath. In Shakespeare too, woman power appears as a literary type. It is the women in his romantic comedies who hold the community together and in the tragedies Desdemona defies the state by marrying a Moor, while the unbending Cordelia refuses to submit to her father's will. Webster's two great heroines, Vittoria Corombona and the Duchess of Malfi represent this new defiant feminism in a patriarchical society.

## The Literary Background

No study of the intellectual, social, political and literary background of the age would be complete without a reference to Seneca and Machiavelli. Seneca's Stoic philosophy did not make so great an impact on the drama of the age though we see its influence in the Duchess's stoic capacity to endure the monstrous tortures that are inflicted on her, or in the last scene of Ford's *The Broken Heart* where news after news of tragedy comes to Calantha and she keeps on dancing without revealing her anguish. It is, however, Seneca's horror stories that appealed to the unsophisticated audience which revelled in watching scenes of blood and thunder. His plays had been translated and published in England between 1559 and 1581 and *Thyestes*, where King Atreus kills the children of his brother Thyestes and serves them up as a feast for his brother—unequalled in horror, even though reported by a messenger—must have thrilled the Elizabethan audience. Sackville and Norton had written their Seneca-type play, *Gorboduc or Ferrex and Porrex* as early as 1561. This was further developed in Kyd's *Spanish Tragedy* and Shakespeare continued the tradition in his tragedies with scenes such as Othello strangling Desdemona and Gloucester's eyes being gouged out on the stage. In all these plays, however (always, excepting Shakespeare), while there was a primitive blood-lust, there was no sophisticated over-refinement into morbid fascination. This, for the many reasons mentioned earlier, became the special prerogative of the Jacobean dramatists.

Machiavelli wrote *Il Principe (The Prince)* in 1530. He was an astute and worldly statesman, essentially amoral and pragmatic.

He had infinite and cynical contempt for the general public and in *The Prince,* he writes, 'One can make this generalisaton about men; they are ungrateful, fickle, liars and deceivers, they shun danger and are greedy for profit.' Virtues are useful to the prudent, he adds, only if he appears to have them. He should appear compassionate, humane, upright and religious, but not be so in his actions and deeds. He must know how to colour his actions and be a great liar and deceive. The only method by which to control the state was ruthlessness. Thus he would be able to manipulate and use people, ultimately for their own good. The political philosophy of prudential exploitation of the weaknesses of human nature to further the well-being of the state was not at all understood by English historians. In English literature Machiavelli was transliterated into a cunning and scheming politician who exploited society for his own selfish aggrandisement. The first English translation appeared in 1640 but by then, Machiavelli's wickedness had already been established in England. The Machiavellian figure merged in the Elizabethan mind with the Senecan tyrant-villain and with the older native Morality figure of Vice. Niccolo Machiavelli also became identified with 'Old Nick', a name for Satan that had existed before Machiavelli's evil reputation reached England. Machiavelli became equally interchangeable with Satan for diabolism. Thus the type of the Machiavellian villain entered Elizabethan and Jacobean drama: Mortimer in *Edward II,* Barabbas in *The Jew of Malta,* Edmund in *King Lear* and Iago in *Othello*. In *The Duchess of Malfi* the Cardinal and Ferdinand have been cast along these lines but above all, Bosola. Bosola, however, is a very complex person and cannot be dismissed just as a character type. Incidentally, Machiavelli had dedicated *The Prince* to Lorenzo de Medici and the English dramatists drew even closer to the exotic setting of Florence and the de Medicis, the world of poison, murder, intrigue and sex.

## Jacobean Tragedy

This combination of Seneca and Machiavelli greatly determined the nature of Jacobean tragedy. A theme that would naturally lend itself to the presentation of violence and murder was that of revenge and 'revenge tragedy' developed into a literary genre.

Revenge is a primitive emotion and it has appeared again and again as a motif in literature. It was there in Scandinavian sagas as also in *Beowulf.* In the sixteenth and seventeenth centuries, the induction of Seneca and Machiavelli gave a new literary flavour to the old theme. The standard plot of revenge tragedies was built around murder that cries for revenge, as in *Spanish Tragedy.* An element of the supernatural would be thrown in or suggested, there would be feigned or actual madness, scenes of horror and murder and, of course, the Machiavellian villain.

The Jacobean stage also gave greater scope to the dramatists to build up the atmosphere of the macabre. From the 'wooden O' that the chorus speaks of in *Henry V* where the stage was empty of props and all was left to the imagination:

> And let us, ciphers to this great accompt.....
> On your imaginary forces work
>
> (*Henry V*, Chorus , 17–18)

Stage presentation became more elaborate and visual aids were frequently used. One reason was that apart from open theatres like the Globe, court entertainment led to the private indoor stage where it was possible to present increased scenic displays and to introduce spectacle, particularly with the help of 'machines' that were designed by such men as Inigo Jones.

Shakespeare used 'spectacle' in some of his later plays and Webster introduces the dead hand and the waxen effigies of Antonio and the children. All this dramatically enhanced the 'atmosphere' of the play. Revenge tragedy developed into a dramatic genre and the theme of blood-for-blood vendetta appears in Kyd's *Spanish Tragedy.* Shakespeare uses it in *Hamlet* and Marston continues with *The Malcontent* and *Antonio's Revenge*. Other plays dealing with this theme follow in quick succession. Chapman wrote *The Revenge of Bussy d'Ambois* and Tourneur *The Revenger's Tragedy.*

Many dramatists, however, abandoned the revenge motif while retaining several of its conventions. The atmosphere evoked by revenge tragedies was very much present, but revenge as an element in the plot was reduced and sometimes disappeared altogether. Tourneur, for example, created the dramatic mood of revenge tragedies while sometimes rejecting the standard plot.

Revenge is present in *The White Devil* where the action of the play develops as a consequence of the murder of Brachiano's wife and Vittoria's husband. The murders are committed by Flamineo, Vittoria's brother. These three, Brachiano and Vittoria primarily and Flamineo their agent, become the objects of revenge. In a sense, therefore, this is a revenge play, but the revenge motif, if central to the plot, is not the centre of dramatic action.

There is no revenge-theme, however, in *The Duchess of Malfi*. That the Duchess has disobeyed her brother's orders that she should not marry or have any relations with men is hardly a situation that calls for revenge. Punishment, may be, punishment for defying orders, but not revenge. It would therefore be incorrect to describe *The Duchess of Malfi* as a revenge play.

Because of the plethora of horrors, of murder and crime, Jacobean tragedy as often been described as melodramatic and sensation-mongering. Violence had also been presented on the Elizabethan stage, but critics have suggested that Jacobean tragedy indulges in the macabre to titillate the audience, that it piles horror upon horror merely to thrill the jaded minds of an age of over-satiation where deeper values have gone and only the appetite has to be gratified. For this reason the tragedy of the age has been described as decadent. The word 'decadence' has been explained in the O.E.D as 'the process of falling away or declining'. The late nineteenth century, the age of the Aesthetes, of Pater and Wilde, has also been described as decadent, though it is far removed from the Jacobean age, and completely different. The Aesthetes openly rejected Arnold's assertion that literature is a criticism of life and declared that moral values were irrelevant in literature and art. The apparent lack of values has led critics to describe the Aesthetes as 'decadent'. But when Wilde wrote in *The Decay of Lying* that 'Art finds her own perfection within and outside of herself' he is actually replacing traditional moral values with aesthetic values. The harshness and brutality of the Jacobean age was of course not here; what we have is the sophisticated urban cynicism of a polished society, but whether it was decadent or not is largely debatable.

In the same way, we should question the so-called decadence of Jacobean tragedy. There is, no doubt, morbidity, there is violence and some dramatists did, at times, indulge in horror for its own sake. We see this, for example, in Ford's *'Tis Pity She's a Whore*, when Giovanni bursts into the banqueting-room holding aloft the smoking and bleeding heart of Annabella on his dagger. There is no real dramatic justification for the excessive horror of this scene, but an age must be judged by the best it produces, not the worst. The peculiarly changing nature of the early seventeenth century has already been discussed, when the security of medieval values had collapsed and the new values were still powerless to be born. Philosophically, man was tossed in a sea of uncertainties and a passionate scepticism was born. If the dramatists had presented a world of peace and harmony, while they were surrounded by confusion and chaos they would have been untrue to their age, untrue to themselves. The sardonic humour of Marston and Chapman and the morbidity that pervades most of the plays of this age, reveal a tortured questioning of life and is not, therefore decadent. Rather, where tragedy slips into tragicomedy, where brutal humour is converted into refined court wit, where sentimentality replaces the lust for life, there the term 'decadent' may be applied. The 'degeneracy' of Jacobean tragedy lies, not in the full-blooded themes of lust, incest and murder, but in the sinking into elegance that was indulged in by some later dramatists.

It is against this background of social, political and philosophical forces, as also the literary context, which includes the influence of Seneca and Machiavelli (bowdlerised) that we must now approach Webster.

# Introduction to the Play

## Life and Works of Webster

It is generally assumed that Webster was born in the latter half of the sixteenth century and the conjectural date of his birth is 1580. The first official reference to him is in 1602, when he was working with a group of hack playwrights under Philip Henslowe, a theatrical manager who employed a number of minor dramatists and who is best-known for his *Diary* which contains valuable information on the theatre, stage and the playwrights of the times.

Webster was the son of a London tailor who also, incidentally owned a fleet of horse-carriages (coaches) and was himself a freeman of the Merchant Taylor's Company. Webster was an odd genius who wrote slowly. He says of himself, 'I confess I do not write with a goose quill winged with two feathers' and he borrowed freely from other writers. In this, he was like other Elizabethan writers who used to keep 'commonplace' books or notebooks where they would jot down striking passages from other people's writings that appealed to them. Webster was particularly notorious in this respect and he has borrowed freely, but always transmitting the passages into his own. He has borrowed freely from Sydney's *Arcadia* and Montaigne's *Essays,* and we find in his plays echoes of many other writers as well, including Chapman and Jonson.

There are innumerable other sources which have been tracked down by recent scholars. The famous passage in *The Duchess of Malfi* (V. v. 5–7) where the Cardinal says:

> When I look into the Fish ponds in the Garden
> Me thinkes I see a thing arm'd with a Rake
> That seems to strike.

was presumed to have been taken from a passage in Lavater's *Of Ghosts and Spirits Walking by Night:* 'Pertinax...... sawe a certayne shadowe in one of his fish ponds......' This has now been traced back to its original source, Capitolinus' life of the vertuous Pertinax. Another famous passage where the Duchess says, early in the death scene,

Th' heaven ore my head, seems made of molten brass
The earth of flaming sulphur, yet I am not mad

echoes a passage in *Deuteronomy* (xxv.iii.23):'And the heaven that is over thy head shall be of brass and the earth that is under thee shall be iron'. William Dent in *John Webster's Borrowing* (University of California Press, Berkeley and Los Angeles, 1960) remarks, 'Excepting Shakespeare, he was the most impressive tragic dramatist of his day. Excepting no one, he was its most impressive borrower'.

Webster was a friend of Dekker, Chapman and Heywood and he began his career with collaborations. He wrote jointly with Dekker in a number of comedies (*Christmas Comes But Once a Year, Westward Hoe,* 1604 and *Northward Hoe*, 1605). He probably wrote an Introduction to Marston's *The Malcontent* when this Boy's Company play was staged at the Globe in 1605. (The play had already been staged at the Blackfriars by the Chapel Boys.)

But all this was basically job work, mediocre in quality. Then after six years of silence he wrote *The White Devil* in 1611 and *The Duchess of Malfi* in 1614—the two most amazing and brilliant tragedies of the Jacobean age. Webster continued to write and his tragicomedy, *The Devil's Law Case* was published in 1623. Appius and Virginia, a tragedy, is commonly attributed to him as also the comedy *Cure for a Cuckold*, but in both cases his authorship has been questioned. These later plays however, are not of any real significance. Webster's fame as a great dramatist rests upon two plays alone—*The White Devil* and *The Duchess of Malfi.*

*The White Devil* was published in 1612 'as acted by the Queen Majesty's Men and there are indications that Webster started working on *The Duchess of Malfi* shortly after. Internal evidence from the text of the play establishes that it was written, or at least part of it, after Chapman's *Seven Penitential Problems*, Donne's *Second Anniversary or The Progress of the Soul* and Thomas Adonis's sermon, *The Gallant Burden* which were all published in 1612. A terminal date for the completion of *The Duchess of Malfi* is October 1614. The play was first published in the Quarto edition of 1623 and in it, the list of actors for the first performance is given. This list includes the name of William Ostler as performing the part of Antonio. Ostler died on 16 October 1614. The play therefore, must have been written before that date. The actual date of the performance is not known but it is likely to have been between the winter of 1613–14 and the middle of 1614.

The setting of *The White Devil* is Rome, afterwards Padua. The action in *The Duchess of Malfi* moves within the orbit of Amalfi, Rome and Milan. Both plays deal with the aristocratic society of Renaissance Italy, both plays reveal corruption, deceit, sycophancy and lust, while murder without compunction, by any means whatever, is a mode of action resorted to again and again.

The protagonist in both plays is a woman, passionate, strong, capable of defying and resisting the oppressive patriarchical norms of the society to which they belong. With Marston may have originated the heroine who is wicked or non-moral and at the same time, fascinating and compelling. The usurper's wife in *The Malcontent* is among the first of these powerful unscrupulous women who dominate with the force of their personality. There is also Marston's *Sophonisba or The Wonder of Women* (1606) and his collaborated (?)play, *The Insatiable Countess* (1613). But we must not forget Shakespeare's Lady Macbeth and Cleopatra.

In *The White Devil* Vittoria Corombona is married to Camillo but in love with Brachiano, whose wife is the sister of Francisco de Medici. Vittoria's brother Flamineo is secretary to Brachiano and in him we have the typical frustrated intellectual already referred to, who has had a good education which has not helped him in the advancement of his career. Brachiano kills Isabella by having poison put on his portrait which she kisses every night while Flamineo contrives to have Camillo killed in a duel.

Vittoria is tried for adultery and murder and sentenced to confinement, from where however, she is carried away and married by Brachiano. Revenge and retribution quickly follow. The Duke of Florence poisons Brachiano and two of his men kill Vittoria and Flamineo, but not before much treachery and many other violent deaths have taken place. The conclusion is one long study of the horror of death presented from every point of view. There is the pathetic incomprehension of Cornelia, Vittoria's mother, over the death of her younger son Marcello, the difficulty and struggle of the intensely alive Brachiano as he dies:

On pain of death, let no man name death to me:
It is a word infinitely terrible.

(*WD*, VIII. iii, 8–9)

There is Flamineo's grotesque

Oh, I smell soot,
Most stinking soot! The chimney is afire

(*WD*, V. vi. 141–2)

There is the superbness of Vittoria's courage:

Yes, I shall welcome death
As princes do some great ambassadors.
I'll meet thy weapon half way (*WD*, V.vi. 220–1)

Vittoria is wicked but magnificent, while her enemies are wicked and mean. Her spirit of ceaseless resistance and fury is astonishing as is her superb wit and arrogance when, in the court scene she mocks at the law that judges her. The Duchess of Malfi is as resolute, as courageous as Vittoria. But while both represent new defiant feminism in a patriarchical society, there is a world of difference between the two magnificent women. While Vittoria partakes of the evil that surrounds her, the Duchess stands apart.

## Sources of the Play

The original source of the story, as with Shakespeare's *Romeo and Juliet* and *Twelfth Night* is Matteo Bandello (1480?–1562) whose multivolume *Novelle* containing 214 racy prose romances was translated into French by Francois de Belleforest as *Histoire Tragique* (1559–82). It is this version, rendered into English by William Painter in *Palace of Pleasure* which is the immediate source of Webster's play. But while Webster adopted Painter's prose romance, he made a number of changes. Antonio had been given a much more prominent position in the original story and a more or less equal weightage had been given to him and the Duchess. Webster placed the Duchess at the centre of all action, making her the tragic protagonist of the play. In the course of the tale Painter had introduced several agents and spies who were engaged by the brothers to keep a watch on their sister and eventually kill her. It is only towards the end, when a Neopolitan gentleman who had been engaged by the Cardinal to kill Antonio delays and keeps changing his mind that the Cardinal selects Bosola. 'This bloody beast was called Daniel de Bosola that had charge of a certaine band of footemen in Milan.' Webster tightens the play by combining all these spies and agents and hired murderers into one single figure. Bosola thus acquires a major and sinister position in the story and Webster fits him into the genre of the Jacobean malcontent. In Painter, Bosola hides in ambush and murders Antonio. Webster has made Bosola a far more complex figure and he accidentally kills Antonio even as he is planning to save him.

In Painter the suspicions of the brothers are aroused only after the birth of the second child and there is no time gap between their getting this news and taking action upon it. In Webster, they get the news of the birth of the first child by the end of Act II and no action is taken till Act III which begins two years later. But in Webster they are present from the beginning and their despotic role in a patriarchical society is established before the wooing and marriage. Thus ominous forebodings of later events hang over the play from the first act and dramatic tension is built up straightaway.

The superb drama of Ferdinand's sudden appearance in the Duchess's chamber is Webster's invention, as are the series of tortures in Act IV, the dumb show at Loretto and the lyrical beauty of the echo scene. The sub-plot of Julia and her sexual relations with Delio, the Cardinal and Bosola are also introduced by Webster, thus heightening the general atmosphere of intrigue, lust and corruption. In Painter, the murder of Antonio takes place more than a year after the Duchess's death. In Webster, the Duchess is strangled at the end of Act IV and there is no time gap as we move on to Act V where Antonio dies by accident. Ferdinand's madness is entirely Webster's invention. This final act is essential to the structure of Webster's play and shows how evil destroys itself and totally disintegrates as soon as the force that resisted it ceases to exist. The characters of the two Arragonian brothers are individualised and the contrast between the cold Cardinal and the fiery Ferdinand enhances the dramatic effectiveness of the play. There is moral disapproval in Painter's delineation of the Duchess's character. He writes of 'the ticklish instigations of her wanton flesh' and describes her as a foolish woman who takes a husband to 'glut her libidinous appetite'. Webster's Duchess has her weaknesses but they are not of a moral nature and there is no moral censure or condemnation.

Webster's original audience could also have been struck by the similarities between Webster's Duchess's life and that of the sixteenth century Duchess of Suffolk who married her steward and had to undergo a number of privations and the travails of travel with her children on the continent as a result of the persecutions she had to face for her Protestantism during Queen Mary's reign. Her story was celebrated in Foxe's *Book of Martyrs* and in ballads and there was a play on her entitled *The Duchess of Suffolk* (1623) on the London stage.

## Plot Construction

The plot of *The Duchess of Malfi* is, in a way, less complicated than that of *The White Devil.* There are five main characters—the Duchess herself, her two brothers the Cardinal and Count Ferdinand, Bosola, the agent whom Ferdinand engages to carry out his wicked designs and Antonio the Duchess's steward, who, by the end of Act I becomes her husband. There are other characters and subsidiary action. But what grips our attention is the story of the Duchess and the forces that are ranged against her. She is a young widow and at the very beginning her two brothers tell her in no uncertain terms that she must maintain her state of widowhood:

> You are a widow
> . . . Let not youth, high promotion, eloquence
> Sway your high blood
>
> (I. i. 298–302)

The Duchess protests, but the Cardinal pronounces a sinister warning:

> The marriage night
> Is the entrance into some prison
>
> (I. i. 329–30)

The authoritative domineering role of the brothers, the self-appointed guardians of the Duchess, indicates the gender relations of a male-dominated society.

The Duchess, however, is made of much sterner stuff and when they leave, perhaps even provoked by them, she defiantly says, 'Shall this move me?' She tells her maid, Cariola, to call her steward, Antonio and in one of the most delicate wooing scenes in literature she offers herself to Antonio and puts a ring on his finger. She then brings out Cariola who, hidden in a recess, has overheard the conversation, and declares that the presence of a witness has made them in the eyes of law, man and wife. Thus ends Act I.

So far the action has moved swiftly, but from now on it progresses in jerks and with gaps and pauses in time. This has caused some critics to comment that though Webster is superb in building up atmosphere and creating powerful scenes, he does not take cognisance of the plot in the ordinary sense of the word. Shakespeare too, has used time gaps, particularly in his last romances but in them there is one big gap as he moves from the dramatic action of one generation to the next

As Time says, in the role of Chorus:

> Impute it not a crime
> To me or my swift passage that I slide
> O'er sixteen years, and leave to the growth untried
> Of that wide gap. (*Winter's Tale*, IV. i. 4–7)

Tomlinson in *Elizabethan and Jacobean Tragedy*[1], remarks that the play is a series of brilliant vignette scenes unrelated to each other. This however, could be a dramatic technique that Webster adopts deliberately. If we carefully study the moments chosen for dramatic presentation we note that they are of crucial significance, bonding the play together. The effect of intense action would have been diluted and dissipated if the play had proceeded upon a steady movement of clock time. Even in the ordinary time chronology of one's own memories it is 'the spots of time' that remain and all the rest fades away. This device, which was adopted by ballad writers of the fifteenth century has been described as the technique of 'episodic intensification' where the spotlight is focussed upon moments of significance against a darkened backdrop. An example of this technique can be seen in the ballad, *Lord Randal*.

[1]T. B. Tomlinson, *Elizabethan and Jacobean Drama*, Cambridge University Press, 1964.

Act I moves swiftly and in one day the action hastens forward to the concluding moment of the Duchess's marriage with Antonio. Then there is a gap of about nine months during which period nothing happens except that the Duchess has conceived. The action of Act II is in two parts with no break in between. Scenes i–iii rush headlong forward with the Duchess giving birth to a son and Bosola accidentally discovering the secret. Without break we move to the second part. In the intervening period Castruchio has travelled to Rome with the news.

There is a long gap of at least two years before Act III begins, because we hear that in the meantime, the Duchess has given birth to two more children. It is this long break that critics have regarded as a defect in plot construction. But the darkened backdrop of two years when dramatic action comes to a standstill heightens, by contrast, the breathless rapidity of movement in the first two acts. Acts III and IV follow each other without break, but the speed of action has here been deliberately slowed down and at the end of Act IV, the Duchess dies. Act V comes almost as an epilogue to the drama of the Duchess.

It is very likely that Webster intentionally manipulates time for dramatic reasons. Rapid action cannot be sustained for very long because this is a strain on the attention of the audience. Perhaps the longest non-stop movement in drama is that contained in Acts I and II of *Macbeth* and here tension in the audience reaches near breaking-point.

The swift course of love and its happy consummation separated by two years from the rest of the play is thus presented as an isolated island of bliss but by the end of Act II—a touch of Sophoclean irony—we know, though the Duchess does not, that the brothers have been informed. Thus to the swiftness is added the hint of fragility and the threat of brevity. Action slows down now and from Act IV the long drawn-out saga of time is always subjective; it moves in diverse paces with diverse people. Time moves fast when we are happy and drags when we are sad. In *The Duchess of Malfi* Webster's control of speed has created this effect.

In Act I we have disconnected pictures of evil and innocence, each moving in its separate orbit. The evil is predatory but the

Duchess's world of love and innocence is secure and unthreatened. In Act II also they are moving in separate orbits but evil has moved closer and is almost impinging on good. One half of the secret has been discovered but what we see in Ferdinand is frustrated and impotent anger, unable to find a victim. The island of happiness is still safe. In Act III evil orbits into the circle of love as Ferdinand steps into the Duchess's room with a dagger in his hand. The eclipse now begins as the brightness of love is increasingly darkened by the world of evil and disruption. The disruption is symbolically repeated within the circle of love itself as the Duchess and Antonio temporarily separate. In Act IV the tortures begin. First the hand, then the waxen effigies of Antonio and the children and finally the choric symphony of madmen. It is these scenes for which Webster has been accused of melodramatic sensation-mongering. But Webster does not present horror for its own sake. He is not titillating the audience. It is the psychological effect the scenes are having on the Duchess rather than the horrors themselves—her tottering sanity, her resilience, her misery, her imprecations on the universe—'I could curse the stars.' And so we come to Act V and the retribution. The vultures that destroyed others now scavenge on each other and kill themselves.

## Imagery of the Play

To try to arrive at some interpretation of Webster's vision of life in this play it is necessary to study the imagery which is pregnant with significance. One set of images stands out clearly, that of scavenging animals and fetid rottenness. At the very beginning of the play Bosola describes the brothers:

> He and his brother are like plum trees that grow crooked over standing pools—none but crows, pies and caterpillars feed on them.
>
> (I.i. 49–52)

Ugly images bespatter the whole play: 'foul black cobwebs', 'horse-dung', 'toads', 'spawn of snake', 'Jew's spittle', 'young children's ordure'. Bestial images of the lowest forms of animal life include 'ulcerous wolf', 'lice and worm', 'hyena', 'scorpions'. In the end Ferdinand is literally turned into a wolf as he falls a victim to lycanthropia.

Again and again characters come vividly to life as others use images to describe them, either in their absence or while they are on stage. The most powerful of these instances is when the Cardinal and Ferdinand read Bosola's news of the birth of a son. They have moved apart from the others and we do not know what they are saying but nothing could be more dramatically effective than the comments of Pescara and Delio as they watch the brothers:

> (The Cardinal) lifts up's nose, like a foul porpoise before a storm
>
> (III.iii. 53)

and the terrible

> The Lord Ferdinand laughs. (III. iii. 54)

the words play directly on our senses. In Act IV when Ferdinand asks Bosola about his confined sister Bosola replies:

> She's sad as one long used to't...
> You may discern the shape of loveliness
> More perfect in her tears than her smiles
> She will muse for hours together.
>
> (IV. i. 3–9)

No stage action could have revealed more exquisitely the Duchess's state of mind. Antonio's own description of her in the first scene reveals her nature and the imagery of light radiates around her.

> She stains the time past, lights the time to come.
>
> (I.i. 214)

Webster's use of imagery does not only reveal character. It emphasises mood and creates atmosphere, it draws our attention to the central action of the play and it foreshadows events to come. The image clusters revolve round certain central themes of the play and their rich suggestiveness recalls Shakespeare. There are repeated images of appearance and reality through which is introduced the motif of hidden corruption that pervades the play. Under the apparent order is revealed a universe disorganised, convulsed and uncertain where chaos reigns supreme. The Duchess herself is caught up in this as, in her terrible curse, she invokes upon chaos to disrupt the whole universe. Related to this are the collective images of melancholy and madness, for madness itself is a disorder, a dislocation, a surrender to chaos. 'Ambition,' says Antonio, 'is a great man's madness', and Cariola, commenting on the breathless rapidity of the Duchess's wooing and marriage says, 'it shows a terrible madness'. Surrounded by lunatics in Act IV the Duchess sees around her a world gone mad—and asks the servant when he announces Bosola's entry, ' Is he mad too?' Yet this is the miracle: she does not lose her sanity.

> I am not mad yet.....
> Th' heaven o'er my head seems made of molten brass
> The earth of flaming sulphur, yet I am not mad.
>
> (IV. ii. 24–6)

Finally, there is Ferdinand who tries to make his sister mad and becomes mad himself.

Images of sex and lust fill the play and much of its action. There is the reptilian coldness of the Cardinal's relationship with Julia and even Delio is not above renewing an earlier affair, while Julia herself is always ready to turn her glad eye everywhere, from Delio to the Cardinal and from the Cardinal to Bosola. The earlier scenes are full of lewd sexual innuendos with Castruchio as the butt of ridicule and the vulgarity of Ferdinand's

> And women like that part which, like the lamprey
> Hath ne'er a bone in it.
>
> (I.i. 341–2)

draws from the shocked Duchess, 'Fie, sir!'

Framed in this sordid setting, like a lily blossoming in a bed of rotting weeds rests the love story of the Duchess and Antonio:

> D. Bless heaven, this sacred Gordian, which let violence
> Never untwine!
> A. And may our sweet affections, like the spheres
> Be still in motion.
> D. Quickening and make
> The like soft music.
>
> (I. i. 485–9)

The imagery is all of heaven and of the music of the spheres. But images of foreboding hover over them because the songs of innocence are always vulnerable. Although the Duchess dismisses Antonio's apprehensions she tells herself:

For I am going into a wilderness,
Where I shall find nor path nor friendly clue
To be my guide.

(I. ii. 364–6)

Two other collective image-clusters repeat themselves throughout the play. One group consists of images of prison and confinement, particularly relevant to the Duchess but also with a universal significance as a comment on human existence itself. The images increase in the second half of the play where the Duchess is physically imprisoned within her palace and symbolically trapped by the evil around her. The picture repeatedly evoked is that of a bird confined. When, in Act III the Duchess and Antonio are banished from Ancona, she contrasts herself to

The birds that live i'th'field
On the wild benefit of nature, live
Happier than we.

(III. v. 18–20)

Bosola compares her to the 'silly birds that are allured to the nets' and the Duchess herself, knowing that she cannot survive long in this state of confinement says

The robin red-breast and the nightingale
Never live long in cages.

(IV. ii. 13–14)

Towards the end Bosola universalises her condition as he says,

Didst thou ever see a lark in a cage? Such is the soul in the body.

(IV. ii. 126–7)

The prison image ultimately dissolves and as death approaches, fades away into images of storm and mist—the storm of living, the mist of uncertainty, the silence of the unknown. They are present in *The White Devil* and repeat themselves in *The Duchess of Malfi*. Vittoria's last words are:

My soul, like to a ship in a black storm,
Is driven, I know not whither.

(*W.D.* V. vi. 247)

And Flamineo says:

> While we look up to Heaven, we confound
> Knowledge with knowledge. Oh, I am in a mist.
>
> (*W.D.* V. vi. 259–60)

In *The Duchess of Malfi* Julia dies with the words, 'I go, I know not whither'. When Malateste asks, 'How came Antonio by his death?' Bosola replies, 'In a mist'. And as death closes around him Flamineo in *The White Devil* says:

> I am i'th'way to study a long silence.
>
> (*W.D.* V. vi. 204)

## The Characters

The discussion of imagery has inevitably included comments on the various characters and it is now time to turn to them. Among the main characters, Antonio is least impressive and his personality pales before the powerful figures of the Cardinal and Ferdinand, the psychologically fascinating Bosola and the Duchess, triumphant in her death.

**Antonio:** Antonio is a good man, but weak, and apt to lose his head in a crisis. His integrity and his belief in discipline, order and harmony are established straightaway in his very first speech. He has just returned from the French court and is full of praise for the way the state is run:

> In seeking to reduce both state and people
> To a fix'd order, their judicious king,
> Begins at home.
>
> (I. i. 5–7)

He is intelligent and perceptive as can be seen in the neat way he sums up the characters of the Cardinal and Ferdinand. His description of the Duchess to Delio reveals his humble and worshipful adoration of the Duchess and when she woos him and unexpected happiness opens up before him, he is overwhelmed. But despite his modesty he is not without ambition.

> Ambition, madam, is a great man's madness. (I. i. 425)

He also enjoys the glamour and the privileges of wealth which he obviously displays because, as he tells Delio, 'they do observe I grow to infinite purchase' (III. i. 28). That he enjoys displaying his wealth indicates a worldly weakness and perhaps this is just as well, otherwise he would have been too much of a cardboard figure of colourful goodness.

But for all his lifelong service to virtue he is weak. He cannot take decisions and at every crisis it is the Duchess who has to tell him how to work out the next plan of action. He is nervous, superstitious and fumbles. When his nose bleeds on the night the Duchess gives birth to her first child, his superstitions get the better of his judgment and in his nervousness he drops the horoscope which gives details of his son's birth. Thus it is his careless fumbling which puts the deadly incriminating information into the hands of Bosola who promptly picks up the paper and sends old Castruchio off post-haste to Rome. Antonio too has his philosophical comment to make on life:

> Heaven fashioned us of nothing, and we strive
> To bring ourselves to nothing.
>
> (III. v. 82–3)

But this remark has nothing original about it and comes as a trite repetition of a much-repeated phrase. The lack of practical wisdom and his foolish goodness lead him to believe that there can still be

> . . . hope of reconcilement
> To the Arragonian brethren? (V. i. 1–2)

He does not deserve a heroic death; he dies by accident, slain by Bosola, mistaken for someone else. Of his genuine love for the Duchess however, there is no doubt, and we recall the hauntingly beautiful lyrical scene of the echoing wall in Act V, sc iii where every remark of his echoes back to him his love for the Duchess and his own imminent death: 'O fly your fate', 'Never see her more', 'Thou are a dead thing'. These echoes sum up Antonio: a shadow and an echo in the monstrous tempest and battle of life.

**The Cardinal:** The two brothers are studies in festering evil, but studies in contrast. The Cardinal is the master-mind, cold and calculating in his moves. He does everything by remote control and has mastered the art to perfection. Ferdinand is merely his tool, adding only his own vicious brand of cruelty to what he has been ordered to do. It is he who plans to use Bosola, but himself remains distant and uninvolved. When Bosola, whom he had formerly used, and who, in consequence has had to serve in the galleys, supplicates him, the Cardinal dismisses him with contempt and scorn, and then instructs Ferdinand:

> Be sure you entertain that Bosola,
> For your intelligence: I would not be seen in't. (I. i. 229–30)

When Ferdinand becomes mad he is anxious lest Ferdinand blurt out the fact of his own involvement and he dissembles to Pescara:

> (Aside) . . . this fellow must not know
> By any means I had intelligence
> In our duchess' death: for, though I counsell'd it,
> The full of all th' engagement seem'd to grow
> From Ferdinand.
>
> (V. ii. 105–9)

It is only when Ferdinand in his madness can no longer act as his agent that he gives direct orders to Bosola. But at the same time he poisons Julia and plans to eliminate Bosola.

But cold and inhuman as he is, he fears retribution and has some sort of primitive sense of the wrongness of evil. His words, as he soliloquises to himself over the nature of hell-fire indicate his guilty conscience and there is something terrifying in his avoidance of the word 'devil' or ' Satan' as he says:

> . . . how tedious is a guilty conscience
> When I look into the fish-pond in my garden,
> Methinks I see a thing arm'd with a rake
> That seems to strike at me.
>
> (V. v. 4–7)

The image that is conjured up is not the bottomless pit of hell but something very ordinary, something very near and homely. Fear of retribution has come close; it has entered his palace and hovers in the very fish ponds in his garden. And at the same time, the object of his fear is faceless, unidentifiable, more terrifying than any visual image of the devil: it is a *thing* armed with a rake.

It is an ironic twist of fate that the Cardinal who had sent others to destruction does so finally to himself. In order to conceal Ferdinand's insanity, he warns Pescara and the others not to come to Ferdinand's aid, and adds that to test them he may 'feign himself in danger' and call them, but they are not to come to him. So, when Bosola attacks him, he cries out in real danger, 'Help! We are betrayed', they disregard what they think is his 'counterfeiting' and Bosola, with mad Ferdinand in his wake, kills him. The whirlgig of time brings its own revenge.

**Ferdinand:** As a contrast to the repellent coldness of his brother Ferdinand is more human, though not any the less despicable. But, as with the Cardinal, there is some conscience within him, and struck with the horror of what he has done, he goes mad. He is a man of passion, of ungovernable passion, incapable of self-control. When he rants and raves at the news that a child has been born to the Duchess, his brother, though equally angry, calmly remonstrates:

> How idly shows this rage which carries you.
> As men convey'd by witches through the air,
> On violent whirlwinds. . . .
>
> (II. v. 49–51)

They are both predatory animals but Ferdinand is, at the same time a prey to his own passions. Despite his fury and perhaps because of it, he does not carry with him any air of authority. The Cardinal gives the general orders, Ferdinand works out the details and Bosola executes. There is not much subtlety in him but there is a curious twist in his mentality which makes him a case study for psychologists.

Both brothers are angry with the Duchess but the birth of a child does not endanger their proprietary rights over her wealth because they do not know that she is married and an illegitimate child poses no threats. Ferdinand's reaction of fury and violence therefore seems disproportionate unless we look for other reasons. When he instructs Bosola to keep an eye over his sister, all he says is

> . . . she's a young widow
> I would not have her marry again.
> Do not you ask the reason: but be satisfied.
> I say I would not.
>
> (I. i. 260–3)

In Act IV, after she is strangled he tries to explain:

> What was the meanness of her match to me?
> Only I must confess, I had a hope,
> Had she continu'd widow, to have gain'd
> An infinite mass of treasure by her death.
>
> (IV. ii. 278–81)

But the explanation rings hollow. For one reason, his initial anger arose when he did not know who her lover was, when he did not think she was married. Another, and perhaps truer, reason may be sought in the language that he uses when he first gets the news of the birth of a child. He uses obscene sexual images that suggest that all he can see in front of him is the figure of a man 'who leaps my sister', of a lecherous father who has committed 'the sin of his back'. It is the sexual act, the consummation of the body's rapture that he is obsessed with. Later, in Act IV when Bosola pleads with him to go no further with the mental tortures,

> And go no further in your cruelty,
> Send her a penitential garment to put on
> Next to her delicate skin. . .
>
> (IV. i. 118–20)

he expostulates:

> Damn her, that body of hers
> While that blood ran pure it was more worth
> Than that which thou wouldst comfort, call'd a soul.
>
> (IV. i. 121–3)

He wishes to protect her delicate skin, her body's beauty; it is only the mind that he wants to destroy 'cause she'll needs be mad'. At the end however, when he sees his strangled sister he realises that he has not after all, destroyed her mind, he has mutilated her incomparable beauty. When someone is strangled, the face becomes convulsed and blue, contorted and bloated, the eyes stare out of their sockets, the tongue protrudes out; it is an ugly sight and Ferdinand cannot bear to look at it:

> Cover her face: mine eyes dazzle; she died young.
>
> (IV. ii. 260)

It is his paranoid fascination for her physical beauty, his frustrated and never-to-be satisfied desire to possess her body and ultimately the realisation that it is this very beauty which he wanted to preserve that he has destroyed, that drives him mad.

Significantly or strangely enough, Ferdinand is alone. His totally sexless life ironically suggests the most perverse of all sexual urges within him (suggested, though never explicitly stated), a repressed and frustrated incestuous sexual desire for his twin sister, the Duchess. The theme of incestuous sex is present, though denounced by society in *'Tis Pity She's a Whore*. But there is such madness and fury in Ferdinand's attitude suggesting 'if I cannot touch her, no one else shall' that one wonders whether what prevents him is not only the sibling relationship but perhaps his own lack of male virility, his own impotence. It is fitting that the bestial abnormality of the man leads to the madness of lycanthropia where he imagines himself to be a prowling wolf, what he really was all his life.

**Bosola:** Psychologically, Bosola is the most complex character in the play and every attempt to penetrate into the real man behind his mask is baffled; he continues to remain a mystery. Outwardly he belongs to the class of the frustrated educated unemployed who have to accept any kind of degrading service to earn his bread. He is an embittered man, railing at the world and railing at himself. Bosola, in fact, fits perfectly into the character-type recurring in Elizabethan and Jacobean literature, that affects the humour of melancholy. We can say 'affects' because while this role gives him relief from his emotions, it seems also a pose which satisfies his ego.

If the melancholy humour is an affectation, what then, is the real Bosola? He is intelligent and very observant and his sharp eyes notice the Duchess's pregnant condition which no one else does: she 'is sick a days, she pukes, her stomach seethes' and she 'wears a loose-bodied gown'. He fulfils his duty as a spy and uses his ingenuity to obtain information which he promptly passes on to Ferdinand. Acting on suspicions and on his own initiative he overpraises Antonio to extract the truth from her.

What do we make of him? A soulless character who, to please his employer obliterates every human consideration from his mind? A sadist who finds pleasure in watching the Duchess's sufferings? A man with no moral sense? A monster in other words? But this is not the impression that we get when he says:

> Oh that to avoid ingratitude
> For the good deed you have done me, I must do
> All the ill man can invent. Thus the devil
> Candies all sins o'er.
>
> (I. i. 278–81)

and he pleads with Ferdinand to go no further with the torture.

But all this does not help us to understand him because everything about him contradicts everything else about him. He loathes what he is doing, yet he does it to perfection. He pities the Duchess, yet finds a kind of pleasure in watching her suffer. He says he will protect Antonio, but one wonders whether he will eventually do so if he feels secure about the Cardinal's patronage. It is only when he overhears the cardinal say of him

> when he hath serv'd my turn
> He dies. (V. iv. 30–1)

it is only then that he determines to save Antonio—and what a botch he makes of it!

Not satisfied with the pose of the malcontent cynic he keeps moving from one role to another, and whichever part he plays, he plays to perfection. He seems to delight in acting. He is the villain and torturer, he is the faithful servant, he is the Duchess's well-wisher, he is a man of pity and compassion, he is the philosopher, he puts on the costume of an Old Man, he calls himself a tomb-maker, and then announces that he is the bellman and intones a doleful dirge. He loves donning the actor's robe. When Ferdinand tells him he must see the duchess he replies, 'Never in my own shape' (IV. i. 134) but one begins to wonder what his own shape is, or whether there is at all, 'his own shape'. He is a faceless person who has lost his own identity or perhaps he has no identity of his own. He exists only in the parts he plays and there is no essential Bosola within. He is an actor par excellence and can emotionally identify himself with any character, he is everything and nothing and is continually filling some other body. He enjoys light and shade, he lives in gusto, be it foul or fair, high or low, rich or poor, mean or elevated. He can delight as much in acting an Iago as an Imogen. The above passage has been adapted from Keats's letter (No. 93) written to Richard Woodhouse on Tuesday, 27th October 1818. Grotesque as the analogy may seem, he approximates to the poet's personality. Herein, perhaps, lies the secret of Bosola's character. He has the 'chameleon' quality of the poet, but he lacks the poet's soul. This is why he is so fascinating and at the same time so frightening. As he dies, he realises that his artist's delight in role-acting his way through life has led to nothing:

> I hold my weary soul in my teeth
> Shalt end in a little point, a kind of nothing. (V. v. 75–9)

**The Duchess:** And so we come to the Duchess who lies at the heart of all the action in the play. In a world of darkness and evil and festering corruption she is a soul that dwells apart and the purity of her nature and of her love for Antonio redeem to a great extent, the meaningless horror of the universe that surrounds her. She is by no means perfect and has her faults. She is warm-hearted but she is self-willed and impulsive and takes decisions entirely on her own judgment. There is, of course, no one she can consult, certainly not her brothers. But she is hasty in her decisions and lacks the cautiousness of maturity:

> let old wives report
> I wink'd and chose a husband.
> (I. i. 353–4)

Tender and womanly as she is, she is, at the same time, the emergent woman who rebels against patriarchical despotism and we admire the strength and courage in defying not only her brother but the norms and codes of the society in which she lives. She is a widow, but refuses to fit into the social construct of how a widow should behave and she is determined not to surrender the pleasures of life and the physical urges of youth. 'Why might I not marry?' (III. ii. 109) she asks, and adds:

> Why should I
> Of all the other princes of the world,
> Be cas'd up like a holy relic? I have youth......
> (III. ii. 137–9)

William Painter, from whom Webster takes the story, disapproved of her on a number of counts. For a widow to marry is wrong; to marry out of class is wrong; to act on her own instinct without consulting anybody is wrong. We note also, an unconscious contradiction in her attitude. She spurns social codes but at the same time is haughtily conscious of her own social status: 'I am Duchess of Malfi still' (IV. ii. 139). But while we recognise these weaknesses which make her only too human and while we realise that the thoughtless rapidity of her action is dangerous, we can only admire her.

Thoughtless and wilfully childish, impulsive and immature: these may have been her faults at the beginning of the play, but she grows through suffering into maturity and into humility and becomes a great tragic figure. She faces all horrors with courage and in crisis and emergency we see the awakening of responsibility as she plans and takes decisions. We see a new mood in her when she says

> naught made me e'er
> Go right but heaven's scourge-stick (III. v. 80–1)

Her brothers are wrong and evil but she learns to recognise that she also is in need of corrective judgment. She bows down before 'heaven's thunder' though she rejects Bosola as the devil that counterfeits it (III. v. 100). She accepts misery, not willingly, but with stoic endurance and with disdain. Only once, when her sufferings reach beyond the point of endurance—and this is her weakest moment—only once does she wish to die: 'I'll starve myself to death' (IV. i. 76) but her innate spirit revives and with all the strength she possesses, she invokes chaos:

> ...I could curse the stars...
> And those three smiling seasons of year
> Into a Russian winter, nay the world
> To its first chaos. (IV. i. 96–9)

Bosola, unmoved, points to the stars: indifferent, pitiless, terrible, 'Look you the stars shine still'. But with the magnificence of her spirit she refuses to yield:

> O, but you must
> Remember, my curse hath a great way to go.
> (IV. i. 100–1)

She now enters her purgatory and having passed through it emerges ready for heaven. She does not yearn for death, nor does she resist it. She accepts it: I perceive death, now I am well awake' (IV. ii. 220) and though she never surrendered to her brothers she now surrenders to death and kneels, with humility, to enter the low-arched gates of heaven. Cariola, her good and loyal waiting-woman, who is killed immediately after, kicks, bites, scratches, pleads and tells desperate lies before they finally strangle her. The heroic acceptance of death by the Duchess, by contrast, further elevates and ennobles her.

Tomlinson in his *Elizabethan and Jacobean Tragedy* has made the interesting observation that innocence, while it struggles to survive in a world of chaos and disorder, draws strength from it and is nourished by it. When the Duchess invokes chaos she is actually identifying herself with it. She is a part of it, not apart from it. It is, however, possible to interpret her nature in a different way. She is what she is because of the opposition of the evil that surrounds her. It is the categorical imperative that she *must* resist evil that makes her strong, that gives her tremendous resilience, and possibly it is her brother's command that she must not marry that instigates her into immediate marriage. In the same way the forces of evil gain their strength and their unity *because* she resists them. What we see here are, in Hegelian terms, two equal and opposite forces maintaining an uneasy tension-filled moment of equilibrium until she is murdered, and immediately the equilibrium snaps. As soon as Ferdinand kills the Duchess and by so doing, destroys the opposite force, there is no longer anything to resist, the strength of evil is dissipated, and in Act V the whole structure collapses.

## Webster's Vision of Life

What is Webster's vision of life in *The Duchess of Malfi*? Evil pervades the play, yet there is also a recognition of good. But does Webster seek or find any resolution to the problem of human existence? There are, perhaps as many interpretations of his philosophy as there are critics. The 'pessimist' school finds in him a nihilistic view of life, a sceptical cynicism, and *The Duchess of Malfi* is a picture of change, confusion and uncertainty. Everything is 'in a mist' and Webster does not perceive anything beyond the chaos of existence. According to David Cecil in *Poets and StoryTellers* (1949) his vision is a moral one and he believes in the ultimate victory of virtue. Irving Ribner in *Jacobean Tragedy: The Quest for Moral Order* (1962) writes, 'the important lesson which Antonio has learned from his wife is how to endure vexation in preparation for his everlasting rest. .......... that the only good in life is the ability to endure life itself.' D.C. Gunby, in his introduction to three plays of Webster sees in the *Duchess* scepticism and at the same time religious belief. The play, to Rupert Brooke (*John Webster and the Elizabethan Drama*), reveals an 'unending soulless energy that heaves and pulses through the lowest forms of life ........ Human beings are writhing maggots in an immense night'. According to Una Ellis-Fermor in *The Jacobean Drama* (1936) evil acknowledges its own nature in the end and the Cardinal redeems himself at last.

Each critic in his own way seeks to find a solution, preferably a moral one, an answer to life. But can the mystery of existence ever be solved? Webster gives us his vision of life; he does not give, and does not have to give, a philosophical explanation of it. He sees a world where destruction, chaos and disorder dominate but he also sees a goodness that resists and never yields. Who wins, who loses, is not his concern.

Shakespeare also sees life as a movement towards destruction but at the end of every tragedy one strong man arises: Malcolm, Fortinbras, Edgar, and order returns and reestablishes itself. There is, however, in the last romances a suggestion of the cyclical pattern of life, that evil will return to be once again overcome by good and this movement will go on. The security of a world that finally survives gives a meaning to the sufferings of mankind in Shakespeare's tragedies. But Webster's is a harsher, sterner (and perhaps truer?) vision of life. He offers no palliatives, no consolation. The jingling couplet at the end of the play:

> Integrity of life is fame's best friend
> Which nobly, beyond death, shall crown the end.

rings false and does not fit in with the harsh vision of life; perhaps Webster added it to please his audience.

At the beginning of the Introduction reference had been made to Conrad's *Heart of Darkness*. Webster's perception of existence in a sense approximates to what Conrad, through Marlowe, perceives in Kurtz. This passage perhaps, is the nearest comment that can be made on Webster's vision of life in *The Duchess of Malfi*.

> I was fascinated. It was as though a veil had been rent. I saw on that ivory face the expression of somber pride, of ruthless power, of craven terror, of an intense and hopeless despair. Did he live his life again in every detail of desire, temptation and surrender during that supreme moment of complete knowledge? He cried in a whisper at some image, some vision—he cried out twice, a cry that was no more than a breath: The horror! The horror!

The picture, however, is still incomplete. Despite this horror, Kurtz leaves a packet of letters for the woman he has loved. Marlowe, while recognising the greatness of a man who has looked fully at life also recognises the essential goodness of goodness and the reality of its existence and that both must exist. When he goes to visit her, he deliberately tells her a lie and conceals from her Kurtz's last words. Marlowe hears from her 'a cry of inconceivable triumph and of unspeakable pain' and we are reminded of the Duchess who dies in the belief that Antonio lives and is reconciled to her brothers. Her last word is 'Mercy'. Marlowe also could not tell Kurtz's beloved the truth: 'I could not tell her. It would have been too dark—too dark altogether.'

Webster thus, recognises that in life both evil and good exist and both have to survive, held together in a tension of opposites, if life itself is to survive.

## Imitations and Subsequent Stage History of *The Duchess of Malfi*

*The Duchess of Malfi* was first published in the Quarto edition of 1613. It was probably completed in the winter of 1613 and 1614 and the first stage presentation was likely to have been around the middle of 1614 (see Introduction, p. xxi).

The most noteworthy imitation is Shirley's *The Cardinal* (1641). The play was modelled on *The Duchess of Malfi* but is far inferior, and the full-blooded plot has been somewhat toned down in deference to Caroline (from Carolus, Latin for Charles) decorum. The two most complex characters, Ferdinand and Bosola, are omitted from the action and the 'sin' of the Duchess's sexual independence is reduced to mere disobedience. She is the widowed daughter-in-law of the King of Navarre and the Cardinal arranges for her to marry Colombo, general of the army. But she loves Count Alvarez. Colombo murders Alvarez and a series of lurid murders takes place. All the action is engineered from the outside and the characters lack verisimilitude. In the end the Cardinal tries to rape the mad Duchess and is murdered by the avenging Hernando, but not before he has succeeded in poisoning the Duchess.

In the season of 1630–31 the King's Men and the Queen's Men between them performed thirty plays at Court. The King's Men, or the King James's Company had already been active under their Elizabethan name, the Lord Chamberlain's Men and had acquired their new name after the accession of James I in 1603. They soon became the most distinguished and the most financially stable of the acting companies and the members, who were actor-shareholders, included Shakespeare, Fletcher, Burbage and Armin. They owned most of Shakespeare's plays, many of Beaumont and Fletcher and of Jonson and also *The Duchess of Malfi*. Records are available of the titles of twenty-one plays given by The King's Men, together with the dates of the performances. *The Duchess of Malfi* was presented in the 'Cockpit in Court' at Whitehall, on 21 December 1630.

During the next thirty years stage performances became very irregular for various reasons. Four times between 1631 and 1641 theatre houses had to be closed down because of the plague. A disturbed political situation followed and on 2 September 1642, the Puritan government passed an ordinance abolishing all playhouses and drama. Surreptitious performances continued at Oxford throughout the war and in 1648 there was a brief reappearance of plays at the Cockpit and Bull in London. But a further parliamentary order put a stop to this and many theatre houses were pulled down, though surreptitious performances still continued.

With the restoration of monarchy in 1660 however, Charles II reopened the theatres and issued a patent to Thomas Killigrew (The King's Company) and Davenant (Duke of York's Company). Thereafter theatre houses flourished, though for a brief period in 1665 they had to be closed down again because of the Great Fire of London.

But by then the tastes of theatre-goers had changed. Their preference was for plays about contemporary sophisticated society, for wit and polish. This paved the way for Restoration Comedy and high tragedy languished.

In the nineteenth century drama was in the doldrums. The subjectivism of the Romantic writers and of the early Victorians was not conducive to serious drama which requires a considerable degree of objectivity and detachment on the part of the dramatist. Shelley's *Prometheus Unbound,* for example, was certainly not meant for the stage. Theatre performance did continue, but full of melodrama and sentiment, catering primarily to popular tastes.

Towards the end of the nineteenth century William Poel brought about a return to the Elizabethan stage and a revival of Elizabethan and Jacobean drama. He broke out of the proscenium frame and introduced an apron stage. In 1894 he founded the Elizabethan Stage Society but even before that in 1892 he produced *The Duchess of Malfi* in collaboration with Greene's Independent Theatre. Sketches in *The Daily Graphic* show the use of a canopied bed, a chair and a dressing mirror (as has been cited in *Notes on Some of William Poel's Stage Productions*, London, 1933).

The next important production of *The Duchess of Malfi* is by the actor-manager, Samuel Phelps. In 1837 he had made his London debut as Shylock at the Haymarket. His contribution to nineteenth-century theatre was in opening the Sadler's Wells Theatre in London, where till now, melodrama had reigned. He ran the theatre for eighteen years (1844–62) and produced thirty-four plays by Shakespeare together with revivals of Stuart drama—Beaumont and Fletcher's *The Maid's Tragedy*, three plays of Massinger and Webster's *The Duchess of Malfi.*

In the last hundred years there have been a number of revivals of Elizabethan and Jacobean drama, but apart from Shakespeare who is an all-time favourite, producers find these plays difficult to present. The modern ear is not well attuned to the nuances of poetic drama and justice is not always done to blank verse which can produce passages of great lyrical beauty and at the same time communicate the dramatic effect of living dialogue.

Reviewers have sometimes reacted unkindly not only to the actual production but even to Webster's *The Duchess of Malfi,* which one reviewer has described as 'a play preposterously incoherent'. In 1919, The Phoenix, an offshoot of the Stage Society, produced *The Duchess of Malfi* at the Lyric Theatre, Hammersmith. The anonymous review, which was published in *The New Statesman* (20 March 1920), while declaring that it is 'a bad play', refers to the beauty of the poetry but adds that the actors 'assassinated' the poetry.

Sixteen years later, in 1935, the play was produced at the Embassy and the review was published in *The New Statesman* on 19 January 1935. The critic is much kinder to the production and speaks well of Joyce Bland who acted the part of the Duchess. The production of George Ryland's in 1945 had John Giegud as Ferdinand and Peggy Ashcroft as the Duchess, both renowned performers of Shakespeare's plays. The well-known drama critic Kenneth Tynan reviewed *The Duchess of Malfi* performed by the Stratford-on-Avon Company at the Aldwych Theatre in 1960. Though he is critical of Webster, he makes the interesting remark that the characters 'come alive the closer they get to death'. This quality of Webster's has already been commented upon in an earlier part of the introduction to this edition. Early in 1971, the Royal Court presented Peter Gill's production of *The Duchess of Malf* which was reviewed by Ronald Bryden in *The Observer* (24 January). Ronald Bryden also reviewed the production of the Royal Shakespeare Society at Stratford later in the same year. He admits that *The Duchess of Malfi* is 'a great play' but that it is 'unactable'. But he also makes the perceptive comment that we have lost today 'the ambivalent Renaissance attitude to greatness as both good and evil, magnificent and dangerous'. Though he is reviewing *The Duchess of Malfi*, this remark is particularly applicable to the character of Vittoria Corombona in *The White Devil.*

## The Text

The first edition of *The Duchess of Malfi* was published in 1623. Three more quarto editions followed in 1640, 1678 and 1708. All three were more or less straight reprints. The present edition has adopted the text of the Revel's edition of *The Duchess of Malfi* (Methuen and Co., 1964) which follows that of the first quarto with the spelling modernised and with minor alterations in the punctuation.

## Dramatis Personae

SCENE: *Malfi, Rome, Loretto, the Countryside near Ancona, and Milan.*

FERDINAND, *Duke of Calabria, twin brother to the Duchess.*
The Cardinal, *their brother.*

DANIEL DE BOSOLA, *returned from imprisonment in the galleys following service for the Cardinal; later the Provisor of Horse to the Duchess, and in the pay of Ferdinand.*

ANTONIO BOLOGNA, *Steward of the Household to the Duchess; later her husband.*

DELIO, *his friend; a courtier.*

CASTRUCHIO, *an old lord; husband of Julia.*

Marquis of PESCARA, *a soldier.*

Count MALATESTE, *a courtier at Rome.*

SILVIO, *a courtier at Malfi and Rome.*

RODERIGO }
GRISOLAN } courtiers at Malfi.

Doctor.

The Duchess of Malfi, *a young widow; later wife of Antonio; sister to the Cardinal and twin sister to Ferdinand.*

CARIOLA, *her waiting-woman.*

JULIA, *wife of Castruchio and mistress of the Cardinal.*

Old Lady, *a midwife.*

Two Pilgrims.

Eight Madmen, *being an Astrologer, Lawyer, Priest, Doctor, English Tailor, Gentleman Usher, Farmer, and Broker.*

Court Officers; Servants; Guards; Executioners; Attendants; Churchmen.

Ladies-in-Waiting.

# The Duchess of Malfi

## ACT I

### Scene i

*Enter* ANTONIO *and* DELIO.

*Delio.* You are welcome to your country, dear Antonio—
You have been long in France, and you return
A very formal Frenchman in your habit.
How do you like the French court?

*Ant.* I admire it—
In seeking to reduce both state and people
To a fix'd order, their judicious king
Begins at home: quits first his royal palace
Of flatt'ring sycophants, of dissolute
And infamous persons—which he sweetly terms
His Master's masterpiece, the work of heaven—
Consid'ring duly, that a prince's court
Is like a common fountain, whence should flow
Pure silver drops in general: but if't chance
Some curs'd example poison't near the head,
*Death, and diseases through the whole land spread.*
And what is't makes this blessed government,
But a most provident Council, who dare freely
Inform him the corruption of the times?
Though some o'th' court hold it presumption

*3.* ***formal:*** correct, exact. *3.* ***habit:*** dress, not behaviour. ***5–15. In seeking...spread:*** Louis XIII was king of France from 1610–13. Though this makes him contemporaneous with the composition of the play, Webster may or may not have any specific king in mind. In any case, Louis XIII would have been only twelve or thirteen and under the regency of his mother, Marie de Media at the time. The idea of a well-governed state probably came from Sir Thomas Elyot's *Image of Governaunce* (1541) viii, and ll. 11–13 clearly echo a passage from Elyot's book: 'the princis palais is like a common fountayne or sprynge to his citie or countrey, whereby the people by the cleannes therof longe preserued in honestie or by the impurenes therof are with sundry vyces corrupted.' ***9. which:*** referring to the royal palace in l. 7. ***13. in general:*** to everybody. ***14. example:*** incident, occasion.

To instruct princes what they ought to do,
It is a noble duty to inform them
What they ought to foresee:—

*Enter* BOSOLA.

Here comes Bosola,
The only court-gall:— yet I observe his railing
Is not for simple love of piety;
Indeed he rails at those things which he wants,
Would be as lecherous, covetous, or proud,
Bloody, or envious, as any man,
If he had means to be so:—

*Enter* CARDINAL.

Here's the cardinal.

*Bos.* I do haunt you still.

*Card.* So.

*Bos.* I have done you
Better service than to be slighted thus:—
Miserable age, where only the reward
Of doing well, is the doing of it.

*Card.* You enforce your merit too much.

*Bos.* I fell into the galleys in your service, where for two years together, I wore two towels instead of a shirt, with a knot on the shoulder, after the fashion of a Roman mantle:— slighted thus? I will thrive some way: blackbirds fatten best in hard weather; why not I, in these dog-days?

*Card.* Would you could become honest.

*Bos.* With all your divinity, do but direct me the way to it— [*Exit* Cardinal.] I have known many travel far for

*23. **court-gall:*** gall means 'sore' but could also mean 'bile which causes bitterness and acidity'. Bosola is both a 'sore' to the court and a railer full of caustic comments on all around him. *29. **haunt:*** wait for or on you, follow you. *31–2. **the reward... of it:*** a common proverb like 'Virtue is its own reward'. *34. **I fell into the galleys:*** Bosola had committed a murder while in the cardinal's service (l. 73) for which he had been sent to the galleys for seven years. *37. **Roman mantle:*** ironically compares the dress of penury with the Roman toga. *39. **dog-days:*** the hottest time of the year in the second half of August when Sirius or the dog-star rose in the sky, often associated with bad times.

it, and yet return as arrant knaves as they went forth, because they carried themselves always along with them;— Are you gone? Some fellows, they say, are possessed with the devil, but this great fellow were able to possess the greatest devil, and make him worse.

*Ant.* He hath denied thee some suit?

*Bos.* He, and his brother, are like plum-trees, that grow crooked over standing pools; they are rich, and o'erladen with fruit, but none but crows, pies, and caterpillars feed on them: could I be one of their flattering panders, I would hang on their ears like a horse-leech till I were full, and then drop off:— I pray leave me. Who would rely upon these miserable dependences, in expectation to be advanced tomorrow? what creature ever fed worse than hoping Tantalus? nor ever died any man more fearfully than he that hoped for a pardon. There are rewards for hawks, and dogs, when they have done us service; but for a soldier, that hazards his limbs in a battle, nothing but a kind of geometry is his last supportation.

*Delio.* Geometry?

***42–5. I… with them:*** one of Webster's many borrowings from Montaigne: 'It was told Socrates that one was no whit amended by his travell: I beleeve it well (saide he) for he carried himselfe with him'. (Florio's tr. I.xxxviii). ***50. standing:*** stagnant. ***53. panders:*** a go-between who caters to someone's illicit or evil designs. Derived from the character Pandarus who acted as a go-between for Troilus and Criseyde in Chaucer's poem. Pandarus originally appeared in Boccaccio's story as Pandare. ***56. dependences:*** subordinate posts. ***58. Tantalus:*** a figure in Greek mythology. He eventually came to represent a man living in hope that is never fulfilled. Tantalus served the flesh of his son Pelops to the gods. As punishment he was sent to Hades where he was condemned to perpetual thirst, standing in a lake of water with fruit hanging above him. Every time he tried to drink the waters receded and the fruit to which he stretched out his hand always eluded his grasp. The word 'tantalising' is derived from him. ***63. geometry:*** see ll. 64–5. Bosola cynically compares a man walking with the aid of crutches to geometrical figures consisting of straight lines and angles. See also ll. 140–2. A famous compass image is seen in Donne's *A Valediction Forbidding Mourning* where he compares lovers to a pair of compasses:

If they be two they are two so.
As stiffe twin compasses are two (ll. 25–6)

The new study of science or natural philosophy had made the use of such mathematical terms popular among writers of the time.

*Bos.* Ay, to hang in a fair pair of slings, take his latter swing in the world upon an honourable pair of crutches, from hospital to hospital—fare ye well sir. And yet do not you scorn us, for places in the court are but like beds in the hospital, where this man's head lies at that man's foot, and so lower, and lower. [*Exit.*]

*Delio.* I knew this fellow seven years in the galleys
For a notorious murder, and 'twas thought
The cardinal suborn'd it: he was releas'd
By the French general, Gaston de Foix,
When he recover'd Naples.

*Ant.* 'Tis great pity
He should be thus neglected—I have heard
He's very valiant: this foul melancholy
Will poison all his goodness, for—I'll tell you—
If too immoderate sleep be truly said
To be an inward rust unto the soul,
It then doth follow want of action
Breeds all black malcontents, and their close rearing,
Like moths in cloth, do hurt for want of wearing.

*Enter* SILVIO, CASTRUCHIO, JULIA, RODERIGO, *and* GRISOLAN.

*Delio.* The presence 'gins to fill—you promis'd me
To make me the partaker of the natures
Of some of your great courtiers.

*Ant.* The Lord Cardinal's
And other strangers', that are now in court?
I shall:—

*Enter* FERDINAND.

Here comes the great Calabrian duke.

*75–6. By the French ... Naples:* The 'recovery' of Naples took place in 1501. Foix was too young at the time and had no part in the action. A historical inaccuracy on the part of Webster. *78–83. melancholy... malcontents:* see Introduction pp.xvi. *85. the presence:* audience chamber.

*Ferd.* Who took the ring oftenest?

*Sil.* Antonio Bologna, my lord.

*Ferd.* Our sister duchess' great master of her household? Give him the jewel:— When shall we leave this sportive action, and fall to action indeed ?

*Cast.* Methinks, my lord, you should not desire to go to war in person.

*Ferd.* Now for some gravity!—why, my lord ?

*Cast.* It is fitting a soldier arise to be a prince, but not necessary a prince descend to be a captain.

*Ferd.* No?

*Cast.* No, my lord, he were far better do it by a deputy.

*Ferd.* Why should he not as well sleep, or eat, by a deputy ? This might take idle, offensive, and base office from him, whereas the other deprives him of honour.

*Cast.* Believe my experience: that realm is never long in quiet, where the ruler is a soldier.

*Ferd.* Thou told'st me thy wife could not endure fighting.

*Cast.* True, my lord.

*Ferd.* And of a jest she broke, of a captain she met full of wounds:— I have forgot it.

*Cast.* She told him, my lord, he was a pitiful fellow, to lie, like the children of Ishmael, all in tents.

*Ferd.* Why, there's a wit were able to undo all the chirurgeons o' the city, for although gallants should quarrel, and had drawn their weapons, and were ready to go to it, yet her persuasions would make them put up.

***90. took the ring:*** a common sport in jousting and tournaments, where a ring was suspended from a post and horsemen riding at full speed had to carry off the ring on a lance. There could be unconscious irony in the use of this word and also 'jewel' (l. 93). At the end of this act Antonio takes a ring from the Duchess. ***95–123. Methinks... often:*** The entire passage is full of sexual innuendos with old Castruchio as the butt of ridicule. ***112. Ishmael:*** According to the Jews, the Arabs were supposed to have descended from Ishmael, the son of Abraham and Hagar (*Genesis,* ch. XXV, 16–18). As desert dwellers they travelled in tents. But 'all in tents' could also apply to the Jews, who are children of Israel, another name of Jacob, also the son of Abraham (*Genesis,* ch. XXXII, 28). Jews have been referred to as tent-dwellers in *Psalm* XXVII, 55. The printer may have wrongly printed Ishmael/Ismail for Israel. ***112. tents:*** A pun may be intended here as surgical dressings were also called 'tents'. ***114. chirurgeons:*** surgeons.

*Cast.* That she would, my lord—

*Ferd.* How do you like my Spanish jennet?

*Rod.* He is all fire.

*Ferd.* I am of Pliny's opinion, I think he was begot by the wind; he runs as if he were ballasted with quicksilver.

*Sil.* True, my lord, he reels from the tilt often.

*Rod., Gris.* Ha, ha, ha!

*Ferd.* Why do you laugh? Methinks you that are courtiers should be my touch-wood, take fire, when I give fire; that is, laugh when I laugh, were the subject never so witty—

*Cast.* True, my lord, I myself have heard a very good jest, and have scorned to seem to have so silly a wit as to understand it.

*Ferd.* But I can laugh at your fool, my lord.

*Cast.* He cannot speak, you know, but he makes faces—my lady cannot abide him.

*Ferd.* No?

*Cast.* Nor endure to be in merry company: for she says too much laughing, and too much company, fills her too full of the wrinkle.

*Ferd.* I would then have a mathematical instrument made for her face, that she might not laugh out of compass:—I shall shortly visit you at Milan, Lord Silvio.

*Sil.* Your grace shall arrive most welcome.

*Ferd.* You are a good horseman, Antonio—you have excellent riders in France; what do you think of good horsemanship?

*Ant.* Nobly, my lord—as out of the Grecian horse issued

*119. **Spanish jennet:*** a light Spanish horse. ***121. Pliny's opinion:*** In *Natural History* (tr. 1601), ch. xlii, Pliny states that 'in Portugal along the river Tagus near Lisbon... that when the west wind bloweth, the mares set up their tails' and conceive from the west wind and 'bring foorth foles as swift as the wind'. ***122. ballasted:*** Ballast causes speed to slow down. But the horse is so lively that, Ferdinand suggests, it is ballasted with *quick* silver. ***132–8. But I can...wrinkle:*** The joke is that while Castruchio is referring to the fool in his household (fools were often congenital idiots) in present company everyone thinks he is a fool. ***140–1. out of compass:*** beyond moderation, a pun relating to the 'mathematical instrument' of the previous line. ***147. Grecian horse:*** a reference to the Trojan horse used by the Greeks to smuggle soldiers into Troy during the Trojan War.

many famous princes, so, out of brave horsemanship, arise the first sparks of growing resolution, that raise the mind to noble action.

*Ferd.* You have bespoke it worthily.

*Enter* Cardinal, Duchess, CARIOLA, [*with* Attendants].

*Sil.* Your brother, the Lord Cardinal, and sister Duchess.

*Card.* Are the galleys come about?

*Gris.* They are, my lord.

*Ferd.* Here's the Lord Silvio, is come to take his leave.

*Delio.* Now sir, your promise: what's that cardinal?
I mean his temper? they say he's a brave fellow,
Will play his five thousand crowns at tennis, dance,
Court ladies, and one that hath fought single combats.

*Ant.* Some such flashes superficially hang on him, for form; but observe his inward character:— he is a melancholy churchman; the spring in his face is nothing but the engendering of toads; where he is jealous of any man, he lays worse plots for them than ever was imposed on Hercules, for he strews in his way flatterers, panders, intelligencers, atheists, and a thousand such political monsters. He should have been Pope; but instead of coming to it by the primitive decency of the church, he did bestow bribes so largely, and so impudently, as if he would have carried it away without heaven's knowledge. Some good he hath done.

*Delio.* You have given too much of him: what's his brother?

*Ant.* The duke there? a most perverse, and turbulent nature:
What appears in him mirth, is merely outside;
If he laugh heartily, it is to laugh
All honesty out of fashion.

*Delio.* Twins?

*157. **brave fellow:*** a dashing gallant, familiar with all courtly accomplishments. *158. **play… crowns:*** indulge in betting. *160. **form:*** outwardly. *164. **jealous:*** suspicious. *165. **Hercules:*** a reference to the twelve labours of Hercules, a mythical Greek hero. *166. **intelligencers:*** spies. *166. **atheists:*** loosely used to refer to people without moral scruples.

*Ant.* In quality:—
He speaks with others' tongues, and hears men's suits
With others' ears; will seem to sleep o'th' bench
Only to entrap offenders in their answers;
Dooms men to death by information,
Rewards by hearsay.

*Delio.* Then the law to him
Is like a foul black cobweb to a spider—
He makes it his dwelling, and a prison
To entangle those shall feed him.

*Ant.* Most true:
He ne'er pays debts, unless they be shrewd turns,
And those he will confess that he doth owe.
Last, for his brother, there, the cardinal—
They that do flatter him most say oracles
Hang at his lips: and verily I believe them;
For the devil speaks in them.
But for their sister, the right noble duchess—
You never fix'd your eye on three fair medals,
Cast in one figure, of so different temper:
For her discourse, it is so full of rapture
You only will begin then to be sorry
When she doth end her speech; and wish, in wonder,
She held it less vain-glory to talk much.
Than you penance to hear her: whilst she speaks,
She throws upon a man so sweet a look,
That it were able raise one to a galliard
That lay in a dead palsy, and to dote
On that sweet countenance: but in that look,
There speaketh so divine a continence
As cuts off all lascivious, and vain hope.
Her days are practis'd in such noble virtue
That sure her nights—nay more, her very sleeps—
Are more in heaven than other ladies' shrifts.

***178. others' tongues:*** acts on advice from tale-bearers. ***186. shrewd turns:*** retaliatory acts of ill-will. ***195. full of rapture:*** delightful. ***201. galliard:*** a lively dance in triple time. ***204. continence:*** self-restraint. A possible pun with 'countenance' in the previous line. ***207. her very sleeps:*** allusion to the belief that dreams reveal the nature of the person. Cf. Donne's 'Who dreamt devoutlier, than most used to pray' (*Progress of the Soul,* ll. 463–4).

Let all sweet ladies break their flatt'ring glasses,
And dress themselves in her.

*Delio.* Fie Antonio,
You play the wire-drawer with her commendations.

*Ant.* I'll case the picture up:—only thus much—
All her particular worth grows to this sum:
She stains the time past, lights the time to come.

*Cari.* You must attend my lady, in the gallery,
Some half an hour hence.

*Ant.* I shall.

*Ferd.* Sister, I have a suit to you:—

*Duch.* To me, sir?

*Ferd.* A gentleman here, Daniel de Bosola;
One that was in the galleys.

*Duch.* Yes, I know him:

*Ferd.* A worthy fellow h'is: pray let me entreat for
The provisorship of your horse.

*Duch.* Your knowledge of him
Commends him, and prefers him.

*Ferd.* Call him hither—
[*Exit* Attendant.]
We now are upon parting: good Lord Silvio,
Do us commend to all our noble friends
At the leaguer.

*Sil.* Sir, I shall.

*Duch.* You are for Milan?

*Sil.* I am:—

*Duch.* Bring the caroches: we'll bring you down to the haven.
[*Exeunt all except* Cardinal *and* FERDINAND.]

*Card.* Be sure you entertain that Bosola
For your intelligence: I would not be seen in't;
And therefore many times I have slighted him
When he did court our furtherance, as this morning.

*Ferd.* Antonio, the great master of her household

***210. And dress...her:*** be guided by her. ***211. play the wire-drawer:*** you exaggerate, spin out your words. ***212. case:*** conclude. ***214. stains:*** eclipses. ***226. leaguer:*** military camp. ***228. caroches:*** stately carriages. ***230. intelligence:*** information. Note that the Cardinal had spurned Bosola earlier in the scene. He does everything by remote control.

Had been far fitter:—

*Card.* You are deceiv'd in him,

*Enter* BOSOLA.

His nature is too honest for such business—
He comes: I'll leave you. [*Exit.*]

*Bos.* I was lur'd to you.

*Ferd.* My brother here, the cardinal, could never
Abide you.

*Bos.* Never since he was in my debt.

*Ferd.* May be some oblique character in your face
Made him suspect you!

*Bos.* Doth he study physiognomy?
There's no more credit to be given to th'face
Than to a sick man's urine, which some call
The physician's whore, because she cozens him:—
He did suspect me wrongfully.

*Ferd.* For that
You must give great men leave to take their times:
Distrust doth cause us seldom be deceiv'd;—
You see, the oft shaking of the cedar-tree
Fastens it more at root.

*Bos.* Yet take heed:
For to suspect a friend unworthily
Instructs him the next way to suspect you,
And prompts him to deceive you.

*Ferd.* There's gold.

*Bos.* So:
What follows? Never rain'd such show'rs as these
Without thunderbolts in the tail of them;
Whose throat must I cut?

*Ferd.* Your inclination to shed blood rides post
Before my occasion to use you:—I give you that
To live i'th' court, here; and observe the duchess,
To note all the particulars of her 'haviour;

***252. rain'd such show'rs:*** a reference to one of the many loves of Jupiter who was also the god of thunderbolts. He visited Danae, imprisoned in a tower in the form of a shower of gold.

What suitors do solicit her for marriage
And whom she best affects: she's a young widow—
I would not have her marry again.

*Bos.* No, sir?

*Ferd.* Do not you ask the reason: but be satisfied,
I say I would not.

*Bos.* It seems you would create me
One of your familiars.

*Ferd.* Familiar! What's that?

*Bos.* Why, a very quaint invisible devil, in flesh:
An intelligencer.

*Ferd.* Such a kind of thriving thing
I would wish thee: and ere long, thou mayst arrive
At a higher place by't.

*Bos.* Take your devils
Which hell calls angels: these curs'd gifts would make
You a corrupter, me an impudent traitor,
And should I take these they'd take me to hell.

*Ferd.* Sir, I'll take nothing from you that I have given:—
There is a place that I procur'd for you
This morning: the provisorship o'th' horse—
Have you heard on't?

*Bos.* No.

*Ferd.* 'Tis yours—is't not worth
thanks?

*Bos.* I would have you curse yourself now,
that your bounty,
Which makes men truly noble, e'er should make
Me a villain: O, that to avoid ingratitude
For the good deed you have done me, I must do
All the ill man can invent! Thus the devil
Candies all sins o'er; and what heaven terms vile,
That names he complimental.

***264. familiars:*** intimate associates. 'Familiar spirit' also meant a devil attendant. See l. 266. ***265. quaint:*** cunning. ***269. angels:*** An angel in Webster's time was a gold coin with the image of St Michael stamped on it. Money, which tempts, is like the devil, hence the play on the words 'devil' and 'angel'. ***280–1. Thus the devil...o'er:*** Cf. *The White Devil* (V. vi. 55–8). 'O the cursed devil/ Which doth present us with all our sins/Thrice candied over'. ***282. complimental:*** elegance or refinement.

*Ferd.* Be yourself:
Keep your old garb of melancholy; 'twill express
You envy those that stand above your reach,
Yet strive not to come near 'em: this will gain
Access to private lodgings, where yourself
May, like a politic dormouse—
*Bos.* As I have seen some
Feed in a lord's dish, half asleep, not seeming
To listen to any talk; and yet these rogues
Have cut his throat in a dream:—what's my place?
The provisorship o'th' horse? say then, my corruption
Grew out of horse-dung: I am your creature.
*Ferd.* Away.
*Bos.* Let good men, for good deeds, covet good fame,
Since place and riches oft are bribes of shame—
Sometimes the devil doth preach. *Exit.*

[*Enter* Duchess *and* Cardinal.]

*Card.* We are to part from you: and your own discretion
Must now be your director.
*Ferd.* You are a widow:
You know already what man is; and therefore
Let not youth, high promotion, eloquence—
*Card.* No, nor anything without the addition, honour,
Sway your high blood.
*Ferd.* Marry! they are most luxurious
Will wed twice.
*Card.* O fie!
*Ferd.* Their livers are more spotted
Than Laban's sheep.
*Duch.* Diamonds are of most value

***287. politic:*** scheming, crafty. ***287. dormouse:*** According to Pliny (*Natural History*), dormice sleep all winter and so renew themselves. Cf. III. i. 21–2. ***296. preach:*** give good advice. ***302. luxurious:*** lascivious. ***303. livers:*** thought to be the seat of passion. ***304. Laban's sheep:*** The story of Laban, father of Leah and Rachel and uncle of Jacob, is told in *Genesis*, xxx, 31–43. Instead of wages Jacob, who worked under Laban, offered to take the spotted and parti-coloured sheep. By a trick he made all the ewes conceive speckled sheep which he then appropriated. Cf. *Merchant of Venice*, I. iii. 75–81.

They say, that have pass'd through most jewellers' hands.
*Ferd.* Whores, by that rule, are precious:—
*Duch.* Will you hear me?
I'll never marry:—
*Card.* So most widows say:
But commonly that motion lasts no longer
Than the turning of an hour-glass—the funeral sermon
And it, end both together.
*Ferd.* Now hear me:
You live in a rank pasture here, i'th' court—
There is a kind of honey-dew that's deadly:
'Twill poison your fame; look to't: be not cunning:
For they whose faces do belie their hearts
Are witches, ere they arrive at twenty years—
Ay: and give the devil suck.
*Duch.* This is terrible good counsel:—
*Ferd.* Hypocrisy is woven of a fine small thread,
Subtler than Vulcan's engine: yet, believe't,
Your darkest actions—nay, your privat'st thoughts
Will come to light.
*Card.* You may flatter yourself,
And take your own choice: privately be married
Under the eaves of night.
*Ferd.* Think't the best voyage
That e'er you made; like the irregular crab,
Which though't goes backward, thinks that it goes right,
Because it goes its own way: but observe,
Such weddings may more properly be said
To be executed, than celebrated.
*Card.* The marriage night
Is the entrance into some prison.
*Ferd.* And those joys,
Those lustful pleasures, are like heavy sleeps
Which do fore-run man's mischief—
*Card.* Fare you well.

***308. motion:*** resolution. ***319. Vulcan:*** an early Roman god of fire and ironsmiths, later identified with Hephaestus. He wove a net of very fine metal ('engine') in which he trapped his erring wife Venus in company with her lover, Mars. ***328. executed:*** pun: (1) carried out (2) resulting in execution (death).

Wisdom begins at the end: remember it. [*Exit.*]
*Duch.* I think this speech between you both was studied,
It came so roundly off.
*Ferd.* You are my sister—
This was my father's poniard: do you see?
I'd be loth to see 't look rusty, 'cause 'twas his:—
I would have you to give o'er these chargeable revels;
A visor and a mask are whispering-rooms
That were ne'er built for goodness: fare ye well:—
And women like that part which, like the lamprey,
Hath ne'er a bone in't.
*Duch.* Fie sir !
*Ferd.* Nay,
I mean the tongue: variety of courtship;—
What cannot a neat knave with a smooth tale
Make a woman believe? Farewell, lusty widow. [*Exit.*]
*Duch.* Shall this move me? If all my royal kindred
Lay in my way unto this marriage,
I'd make them my low footsteps: and even now,
Even in this hate, as men in some great battles,
By apprehending danger, have achiev'd
Almost impossible actions—I have heard soldiers say so—
So I, through frights, and threat'nings, will assay
This dangerous venture: let old wives report
I wink'd and chose a husband. Cariola,

[*Enter* CARIOLA.]

To thy known secrecy I have given up
More than my life, my fame:—
*Cari.* Both shall be safe:
For I'll conceal this secret from the world
As warily as those that trade in poison
Keep poison from their children.

***333. wisdom…end:*** wisdom lies in anticipating the consequences or end of action. ***338. chargeable:*** expensive. ***341. lamprey:*** eel-like fish with no bones. An obscene sexual innuendo which he quickly alters by saying that he is referring to the tongue. ***348. footsteps:*** rungs of a ladder. ***354. wink'd:*** shut my eyes.

*Duch.* Thy protestation
Is ingenious and hearty: I believe it.
Is Antonio come?
*Cari.* He attends you:—
*Duch.* Good dear soul,
Leave me: but place thyself behind the arras,
Where thou mayst overhear us:—
wish me good speed
For I am going into a wilderness,
Where I shall find nor path, nor friendly clew
To be my guide. [*Cariola withdraws behind the arras.*]

[*Enter* ANTONIO.]

I sent for you—sit down:
Take pen and ink, and write: are you ready?
*Ant.* Yes:—
*Duch.* What did I say?
*Ant.* That I should write somewhat.
*Duch.* O, I remember:—
After these triumphs, and this large expense,
It's fit, like thrifty husbands, we inquire
What's laid up for tomorrow.
*Ant.* So please your beauteous excellence.
*Duch.* Beauteous ?
Indeed I thank you: I look young for your sake.
You have ta'en my cares upon you.
*Ant.* I'll fetch your grace
The particulars of your revenue, and expense.
*Duch.* O, you are an upright treasurer: but you mistook,
For when I said I meant to make inquiry

***360. ingenious and hearty:*** intelligent and straight from the heart, sincere. ***365. clew:*** clue. ***366–508.*** The wooing scene. An amusing instance of a steward aspiring for the hand of his mistress, though totally incongruous in this context is seen in *Twelfth Night* when Malvolio says, 'There is example for 't. The Lady of Strachey married the yeoman of the wardrobe'. The 'example' however, was probably invented by Shakespeare so that Malvolio could justify his case to himself, because no historical or literary allusion has been traced to the Lady of Strachey. ***370. triumphs:*** festivities. ***371. husbands:*** managers of households. Cf. husbandry, thrift. But in l. 387 'husband' has the modern meaning.

What's laid up for tomorrow, I did mean
What's laid up yonder for me.

*Ant.* Where?

*Duch.* In heaven—
I am making my will (as 'tis fit princes should,
In perfect memory), and I pray sir, tell me
Were not one better make it smiling, thus,
Than in deep groans, and terrible ghastly looks,
As if the gifts we parted with procur'd
That violent distraction?

*Ant.* O, much better.

*Duch.* If I had a husband now, this care were quit:
But I intend to make you overseer;—
What good deed shall we first remember? say.

*Ant.* Begin with that first good deed began i'th' world
After man's creation, the sacrament of marriage—
I'd have you first provide for a good husband,
Give him all.

*Duch.* All?

*Ant.* Yes, your excellent self.

*Duch.* In a winding sheet?

*Ant.* In a couple.

*Duch.* Saint Winifred, that were a strange will!

*Ant.* 'Twere strange if there were no will in you
To marry again.

*Duch.* What do you think of marriage?

*Ant.* I take't, as those that deny purgatory—
It locally contains, or heaven, or hell;
There's no third place in't.

*Duch.* How do you affect it?

*Ant.* My banishment, feeding my melancholy,
Would often reason thus . . .

*Duch.* Pray let's hear it.

*Ant.* Say a man never marry, nor have children,

***394. winding-sheet:*** pun: (1) a bedsheet for lovers (2) in which dead people are wrapped. The second meaning is ominously ironic. ***394. couple:*** (1) two sheets (2) wedlock couple. ***395. Saint Winifred:*** a 7th century Welsh saint and patron of virgins. ***395. will:*** (1) inclination (2) passion (3) legal testament.

What takes that from him? only the bare name
Of being a father, or the weak delight
To see the little wanton ride a-cock-horse
Upon a painted stick, or hear him chatter
Like a taught starling.

*Duch.* Fie, fie, what's all this?
One of your eyes is blood-shot—use my ring to't,
They say 'tis very sovereign—'twas my wedding ring,
And I did vow never to part with it,
But to my second husband.

*Ant.* You have parted with it now.

*Duch.* Yes, to help your eyesight.

*Ant.* You have made me stark blind.

*Duch.* How?

*Ant.* There is a saucy, and ambitious devil
Is dancing in this circle.

*Duch.* Remove him.

*Ant.* How ?

*Duch.* There needs small conjuration, when your finger
May do it: thus—is it fit?
[*She puts her ring upon his finger:*] *he kneels.*

*Ant.* What said you?

*Duch.* Sir,
This goodly roof of yours is too low built,
I cannot stand upright in't, nor discourse,
Without I raise it higher: raise yourself,
Or if you please, my hand to help you: so. [*Raises him.*]

*Ant.* Ambition, madam, is a great man's madness,
That is not kept in chains, and close-pent rooms,
But in fair lightsome lodgings, and is girt
With the wild noise of prattling visitants,
Which makes it lunatic, beyond all cure—
Conceive not I am so stupid but I aim
Whereto your favours tend: but he's a fool
That, being a-cold, would thrust his hands i'th' fire

***404. what...him:*** what does he lose. ***406.wanton:*** term of affection. ***410. sovereign:*** effective. ***425–9. Ambition...cure:*** Ambition is associated with great men surrounded by flatterers, and ambition can drive one mad. The first of many references to madness, which is a recurring motif in the play. ***430. aim:*** guess, understand.

To warm them.
*Duch.* So, now the ground's broke,
You may discover what a wealthy mine
I make you lord of.
*Ant.* O, my unworthiness !
*Duch.* You were ill to sell yourself—
This dark'ning of your worth is not like that
Which tradesmen use i'th' city; their false lights
Are to rid bad wares off: and I must tell you
If you will know where breathes a complete man—
I speak it without flattery—turn your eyes
And progress through yourself.
*Ant.* Were there nor heaven nor hell,
I should be honest: I have long serv'd virtue,
And ne'er ta'en wages of her.
*Duch.* Now she pays it !
The misery of us that are born great—
We are forc'd to woo, because none dare woo us:
And as a tyrant doubles with his words,
And fearfully equivocates, so we
Are forc'd to express our violent passions
In riddles, and in dreams, and leave the path
Of simple virtue, which was never made
To seem the thing it is not. Go, go brag
You have left me heartless—mine is in your bosom,
I hope 'twill multiply love there. You do tremble:
Make not your heart so dead a piece of flesh
To fear, more than to love me: sir, be confident—
What is't distracts you? This is flesh, and blood, sir;
'Tis not the figure cut in alabaster
Kneels at my husband's tomb. Awake, awake, man!
I do here put off all vain ceremony,
And only do appear to you a young widow
That claims you for her husband, and like a widow,
I use but half a blush in't.
*Ant.* Truth speak for me:

***437–42. This dark'ning…yourself:*** You underrate yourself, assess your true worth.
***459. alabaster:*** Cf. *M of V.* I. 183: 'Why should a man, whose blood is warm within/Sit like his grandsire, cut in alabaster?'

I will remain the constant sanctuary
Of your good name.

*Duch.* I thank you, gentle love,
And 'cause you shall not come to me in debt,
Being now my steward, here upon your lips
I sign your *Quietus est*:— [*Kisses him.*]
This you should have begg'd now—
I have seen children oft eat sweetmeats thus,
As fearful to devour them too soon.

*Ant.* But for your brothers?

*Duch.* Do not think of them—
All discord, without this circumference,
Is only to be pitied, and not fear'd:
Yet, should they know it, time will easily
Scatter the tempest.

*Ant.* These words should be mine,
And all the parts you have spoke, if some part of it
Would not have savour'd flattery.

*Duch.* Kneel. [CARIOLA *comes from behind the arras.*]

*Ant.* Hah?

*Duch.* Be not amaz'd, this woman's of my counsel—
I have heard lawyers say, a contract in a chamber
*Per verba de presenti* is absolute marriage:—
Bless, heaven, this sacred Gordian, which let violence
Never untwine.

*Ant.* And may our sweet affections, like the spheres,
Be still in motion.

*Duch.* Quickening, and make

***469. Quietus est:*** a legal term meaning 'discharged', but also used to mean 'death'. Cf. *Hamlet* III. 175. ***474. circumference:*** They have now embraced; outside the circle of their arms. ***484. per...presenti:*** Latin phrase meaning 'by words concerning the present'. When a couple declared themselves to be man and wife, this was recognised as a legal marriage, but without the sanctity of a church wedding. ***485. Gordian:*** A Greek legend of King Gordius of Phrygia. He tied a knot in the yoke of the oxen that pulled his chariot. An oracle had declared that whoever unravelled it would rule Asia. Alexander the Great cut through the knot. ***487–9. the spheres...soft music:*** This refers to the belief that spheres (heavenly bodies) perpetually moving round the earth produced heavenly music which ordinary mortals could not hear. Cf. *M. of V.* v. i. 60–3.

There's not the smallest orb which thou behold'st
But in his motion like an angel sings
Still quiring to the young-eyed cherubims.

The like soft music.
*Ant.* That we may imitate the loving palms,
Best emblem of a peaceful marriage,
That ne'er bore fruit, divided.
*Duch.* What can the church force more?
*Ant.* That Fortune may not know an accident,
Either of joy or sorrow, to divide
Our fixed wishes.
*Duch.* How can the church bind faster ?
We now are man and wife, and 'tis the church
That must but echo this:—maid, stand apart—
I now am blind.
*Ant.* What's your conceit in this?
*Duch.* I would have you lead your fortune by the hand,
Unto your marriage bed:—
(You speak in me this, for we now are one)
We'll only lie, and talk together, and plot
T'appease my humorous kindred; and if you please,
Like the old tale, in 'Alexander and Lodowick',
Lay a naked sword between us, keep us chaste:—
O, let me shroud my blushes in your bosom,
Since 'tis the treasury of all my secrets.

[*Exeunt* Duchess *and* ANTONIO.]

*Cari.* Whether the spirit of greatness or of woman
Reign most in her, I know not, but it shows
A fearful madness; I owe her much of pity. *Exit.*

***490. loving palms:*** a common idea at the time, derived from Pliny's *Natural History*. ***499. What's your conceit in this?:*** What do you mean? ***504. humorous:*** ill-humoured. ***505. Alexander and Lodowick:*** Two friends who looked exactly alike. Lodowick married the Princess of Hungary in Alexander's name and placed a sword between him and the Princess so that his friend might not be wronged. This story was well-known and made into a ballad. ***511. a fearful madness:*** prophetic words. Count Ferdinand tries to drive his sister mad, but eventually becomes mad himself.

# ACT II

## Scene i

*Enter* BOSOLA *and* CASTRUCHIO.

*Bos.* You say you would fain be taken for an eminent courtier?

*Cast.* 'Tis the very main of my ambition.

*Bos.* Let me see, you have a reasonable good face for't already, and your night-cap expresses your ears sufficient largely—I would have you learn to twirl the strings of your band with a good grace; and in a set speech, at th' end of every sentence, to hum, three or four times, or blow your nose till it smart again, to recover your memory; when you come to be a president in criminal causes, if you smile upon a prisoner, hang him, but if you frown upon him and threaten him, let him be sure to 'scape the gallows.

*Cast.* I would be a very merry president—.

*Bos.* Do not sup o'nights, 'twill beget you an admirable wit.

*Cast.* Rather it would make me have a good stomach to quarrel, for they say your roaring boys eat meat seldom, and that makes them so valiant. But how shall I know whether the people take me for an eminent fellow?

*Bos.* I will teach a trick to know it: give out you lie a-dying, and if you hear the common people curse you, be sure you are taken for one of the prime night-caps—

*Enter an* Old Lady.

***2. main:*** main purpose. ***4. ears:*** Castruchio is old and foolish and is the butt of jokes in this scene as earlier in Act I. The reference is to the large ears of an ass. Castruchio is also a cuckold (his wife is the Cardinal's mistress) and though cuckolds are usually shown as having horns, sometimes they are represented with large ears. ***6. band:*** This could refer to the latest fashion at court or to a lawyer's tabs because Castruchio claims he is a lawyer. Lawyers are also sometimes referred to as 'night caps'. ***23.* Stage Directions. *Enter an old lady*:** She will later act as midwife.

You come from painting now?

*Old lady.* From what?

*Bos.* Why, from your scurvy face-physic—to behold thee not painted inclines somewhat near a miracle: these, in thy face here, were deep ruts and foul sloughs the last progress. There was a lady in France, that having had the smallpox, flayed the skin off her face to make it more level; and whereas before she looked like a nutmeg-grater, after she resembled an abortive hedgehog.

*Old Lady.* Do you call this painting?

*Bos.* No, no, but careening of an old morphewed lady, to make her disembogue again—there's rough-cast phrase to your plastic.

*Old Lady.* It seems you are well acquainted with my closet.

*Bos.* One would suspect it for a shop of witchcraft, to find in it the fat of serpents, spawn of snakes, Jews' spittle, and their young children's ordure—and all these for the face: I would sooner eat a dead pigeon, taken from the soles of the feet of one sick of the plague, than kiss one of you fasting. Here are two of you, whose sin of your youth is the very patrimony of the physician, makes him renew his footcloth with the spring and change his high-prized courtezan with the fall of the leaf: I do wonder you do not loathe yourselves—observe my meditation now:

What thing is in this outward form of man
To be belov'd? we account it ominous
If nature do produce a colt, or lamb,
A fawn, or goat, in any limb resembling
A man; and fly from't as a prodigy.
Man stands amaz'd to see his deformity
In any other creature but himself.
But in our own flesh, though we bear diseases

***23. painting:*** applying make-up on her face. So also 'face-physic' in l. 25. ***27. ruts:*** wrinkles. ***34. careening:*** a term used for ships that were tilted over for scraping and cleaning. ***34. morphewed:*** scabby. ***35. disembogue:*** a term for emptying out the water from the ship's hold. ***35. rough-cast:*** rough plaster. ***44. patrimony:*** inheritance. Physicians earn a lot from attending to old people.

Which have their true names only ta'en from beasts,
As the most ulcerous wolf, and swinish measle;
Though we are eaten up of lice and worms,
And though continually we bear about us
A rotten and dead body, we delight
To hide it in rich tissue: all our fear—
Nay, all our terror—is lest our physician
Should put us in the ground, to be made sweet.
Your wife's gone to Rome: you two couple,
  and get you
To the wells at Lucca, to recover your aches.
[*Exeunt* CASTRUCHIO *and* Old Lady.]
I have other work on foot:—I observe our duchess
Is sick o' days, she pukes, her stomach seethes,
The fins of her eyelids look most teeming blue,
She wanes i'th' cheek, and waxes fat i'th'flank;
And (contrary to our Italian fashion)
Wears a loose-body'd gown—there's somewhat in't!
I have a trick may chance discover it,
A pretty one: I have bought some apricocks,
The first our spring yields.

*Enter* ANTONIO *and* DELIO [*talking apart*].

*Delio.* And so long since married?
You amaze me.

*Ant.* Let me seal your lips for ever,
For did I think that anything but th' air
Could carry these words from you, I should wish
You had no breath at all:—
[*To Bosola*] Now sir, in your contemplation?
You are studying to become a great wise fellow?

*Bos.* O sir, the opinion of wisdom is a foul tetter that runs all over a man's body: if simplicity direct us to have no evil, it directs us to a happy being;

***58. ulcerous...measle:*** Names of animals were sometimes used to describe certain diseases. ***66. Lucca:*** a spa or mineral spring in Italy famous for its baths in the $16^{\text{th}}$ and $17^{\text{th}}$ centuries. ***69. fins:*** the edges of her eyelids. ***74. apricocks:*** apricots. ***82. opinion... wisdom:*** adapted from Florio's translation of Montaigne's *Essays,* II, xii. ***82. tetter:*** sore.

for the subtlest folly proceeds from the subtlest wisdom: let me be simply honest.

*Ant.* I do understand your inside.

*Bos.* Do you so?

*Ant.* Because you would not seem to appear to the world puffed up with your preferment, you continue this out-of-fashion melancholy—leave it, leave it.

*Bos.* Give me leave to be honest in any phrase, in any compliment whatsoever—shall I confess myself to you? I look no higher than I can reach: they are the gods that must ride on winged horses; a lawyer's mule of a slow pace will both suit my disposition and business: for mark me, when a man's mind rides faster than his horse can gallop, they quickly both tire.

*Ant.* You would look up to heaven, but I think
The devil, that rules i'th' air, stands in your light.

*Bos.* O sir, you are lord of the ascendant, chief man with the duchess, a duke was your cousin-german removed:—say you were lineally descended from King Pepin, or he himself, what of this? search the heads of the greatest rivers in the world, you shall find them but bubbles of water. Some would think the souls of princes were brought forth by some more weighty cause than those of meaner persons—they are deceived, there's the same hand to them: the like passions sway them, the same reason that makes a vicar go to law for a tithe-pig and undo his neighbours, makes them

***91. out-of-fashion melancholy:*** an ironical dig at Bosola's new status in the Duchess's household and at the humour of melancholy which he affects and which is usually a pose for disgruntled people. He need not be disgruntled now. ***92–9. Give me leave... tire:*** Bosola countercharges by implying that Antonio is also ambitious. ***94–5. they are... winged horses:*** adapted from Florio, I. xlii. ***98. his horse... gallop:*** another dig at Antonio who is noted for his horsemanship. ***102. lord... ascendant:*** any planet within the zodiacal house of the sky that is rising in the east, which is powerful at that time. Unconscious irony because Antonio's son is born in the same scene and his horoscope foretells a violent death (II.iii.64–5). ***103. cousin-german removed:*** first cousin once removed. ***105. King Pepin:*** Probably Pepin the Short (c. 714–68) first Carolingian king of the Franks and father of Charlemagne. ***108–15. Some... cannon:*** adapted from Florio II. xi.

spoil a whole province, and batter down goodly
cities with the cannon.

*Enter* Duchess [*with* Attendants *and* Ladies.]

*Duch.* Your arm Antonio—do I not grow fat?
I am exceeding short-winded:—Bosola,
I would have you, sir, provide for me a litter,
Such a one as the Duchess of Florence rode in.

*Bos.* The duchess us'd one when she was great with child.

*Duch.* I think she did:—Come hither, mend my ruff—
Here, when? thou art such a tedious lady; and
Thy breath smells of lemon pills—would thou hadst done—
Shall I swoon under thy fingers? I am
So troubled with the mother.

*Bos.* [*Aside*] I fear too much.

*Duch.* I have heard you say that the French courtiers
Wear their hats on 'fore the king.

*Ant.* I have seen it.

*Duch.* In the presence?

*Ant.* Yes:—

*Duch.* Why should not we bring up that fashion?
'Tis ceremony more than duty, that consists
In the removing of a piece of felt:
Be you the example to the rest o' th' court,
Put on your hat first.

*Ant.* You must pardon me:
I have seen, in colder countries than in France,
Nobles stand bare to th' prince; and the distinction
Methought show'd reverently.

*Bos.* I have a present for your grace.

*Duch.* For me sir?

***119. Duchess of Florence:*** The particular reference has not been traced by editors. ***120. The Duchess...child:*** Bosola's remark is deliberately suggestive. ***121–4. Come hither... fingers:*** The Duchess's impatience is the result of her physical condition. ***123. pills:*** peel or rind. ***124. swoon:*** The original Quarto 'sound' was emended by Dyce to 'swoon'. ***125. mother:*** a common word for hysteria. A pun because she is about to become a mother. ***126–7. I have heard...king:*** Antonio has recently returned from France. ***128. in the presence:*** audience-chamber.

*Bos.* Apricocks, madam.
*Duch.* O sir, where are they?
I have heard of none to-year.
*Bos.* [*Aside*] Good, her colour rises.
*Duch.* Indeed I thank you; they are wondrous fair ones:
What an unskilful fellow is our gardener!
We shall have none this month.
*Bos.* Will not your grace pare them?
*Duch.* No, they taste of musk, methinks;
indeed they do:—
*Bos.* I know not: yet I wish your grace had par'd 'em:—
*Duch.* Why?
*Bos.* I forgot to tell you the knave gard'ner
(Only to raise his profit by them the sooner)
Did ripen them in horse-dung.
*Duch.* O you jest:—
You shall judge; pray taste one.
*Ant.* Indeed madam,
I do not love the fruit.
*Duch.* Sir, you are loth
To rob us of our dainties:—'tis a delicate fruit,
They say they are restorative.
*Bos.* 'Tis a pretty art,
This grafting.
*Duch.* 'Tis so: a bettering of nature.
*Bos.* To make a pippin grow upon a crab,
A damson on a blackthorn:— [*Aside*] how greedily
she eats them!
A whirlwind strike off these bawd farthingales,
For, but for that, and the loose-body'd gown,
I should have discover'd apparently
The young springal cutting a caper in her belly.
*Duch.* I thank you, Bosola, they were right good ones—
If they do not make me sick.

***139. to-year:*** this year. ***148. horse-dung:*** A possible sexual innuendo. The Duchess, he suspects, has mated with someone of inferior status. ***151–3. dainties ...grafting:*** more sexual innuendos. ***154–5. pippin...blackthorn:*** The pippin is considered to be superior to crab-apple and the damson fruit to blackthorn berry. ***156. farthingales:*** hooped petticoats. ***158. apparently:*** openly, visibly. ***159. springal:*** the child (in her womb).

*Ant.* How now madam ?
*Duch.* This green fruit and my stomach are not friends—
How they swell me!
*Best.* [*Aside*] Nay, you are too much swell'd already.
*Duch.* O, I am in an extreme cold sweat!
*Bos.* I am very sorry:—
*Duch.* Lights to my chamber: O good Antonio,
I fear I am undone. *Exit.*
*Delio.* Lights there, lights!
[*Exeunt all except* ANTONIO *and* DELIO.]
*Ant.* O my most trusty Delio, we are lost !
I fear she's fall'n in labour; and there's left
No time for her remove.
*Delio.* Have you prepar'd
Those ladies to attend her? and procur'd
That politic safe conveyance for the midwife
Your duchess plotted?
*Ant.* I have:—
*Delio.* Make use then of this forc'd occasion:
Give out that Bosola hath poison'd her
With these apricocks; that will give some colour
For her keeping close.
*Ant.* Fie, fie, the physicians
Will then flock to her.
*Delio.* For that you may pretend
She'll use some prepar'd antidote of her own,
Lest the physicians should re-poison her.
*Ant.* I am lost in amazement: I know not what to think on't.
*Exeunt.*

***176. colour:*** excuse.

## Scene ii.

*Enter* BOSOLA.

*Bos.* So, so: there's no question but her tetchiness and most vulturous eating of the apricocks are apparent signs of breeding—

*Enter* Old Lady.

Now?

*Old Lady.* I am in haste, sir.

*Bos.* There was a young waiting-woman had a monstrous desire to see the glass-house.

*Old Lady.* Nay, pray let me go:—

*Bos.* And it was only to know what strange instrument it was should swell up a glass to the fashion of a woman's belly.

*Old Lady.* I will hear no more of the glass-house—you are still abusing women!

*Bos.* Who I? no, only (by the way now and then) mention your frailties. The orange tree bears ripe and green fruit, and blossoms all together: and some of you give entertainment for pure love; but more, for more precious reward. The lusty spring smells well; but drooping autumn tastes well: if we have the same golden showers that rained in the time of Jupiter the Thunderer, you have the same Danäes still, to hold up their laps to receive them:—didst thou never study the mathematics?

*Old Lady.* What's that, sir?

*Bos.* Why, to know the trick how to make a many lines meet in one centre:—go, go; give your foster-daughters good counsel; tell them that the devil takes

***1. tetchiness:*** irritability. ***6–29. There was…time passes:*** Bosola deliberately delays her, guessing the reason for her haste. ***7. glass-house:*** glass-blowing factory. Blown glass is here likened to a pregnant woman's belly. See l. 10. ***22. Danäes:*** See note to I. i. 252.

delight to hang at a woman's girdle, like a false rusty watch, that she cannot discern how the time passes.

[*Exit* Old Lady.]

*Enter* ANTONIO, DELIO, RODERIGO, GRISOLAN.

*Ant.* Shut up the court gates:—

*Rod.* Why sir? what's the danger?

*Ant.* Shut up the posterns presently: and call
All the officers o 'th' court.

*Gris.* I shall instantly. [*Exit.*]

*Ant.* Who keeps the key o' th' park gate?

*Rod.* Forobosco.

*Ant.* Let him bring 't presently.

*Enter* [GRISOLAN *with*] Officers.

*1st. Off.* O, gentlemen o' th' court, the foulest treason!

*Bos.* [*Aside*] If that these apricocks should be posion'd now,
Without my knowledge!

*1st. Off.* There was taken even now a Switzer in the duchess' bedchamber.

*2nd.Off.* A Switzer?

*1st Off.* With a pistol in his great cod-piece.

*Bos.* Ha, ha, ha !

*1st. Off.* The cod-piece was the case for't.

*2nd. Off.* There was a cunning traitor. Who would have searched his cod-piece?

*1st. Off.* True, if he had kept out of the ladies' chambers:—and all the moulds of his buttons were leaden bullets.

*2nd. Off.* O, wicked cannibal! a fire-lock in's cod-piece !

*1st. Off.* 'Twas a French plot, upon my life.

*2nd. Off.* To see what the devil can do!

*Ant.* All the officers here?

*Off.* We are:—

***38. Switzer:*** Swiss mercenary soldier. ***41. with a...cod-piece:*** The cod-piece is an ornamental flap attached to the front of a tight-fitting breeches and was a necessary dress accessory in the 16th century. The passage is loaded with bawdy sexual innuendos. There is possibly a pun on the word 'pistol', pronounced 'pizzle', another word for 'penis'. ***49. French:*** The French were considered to be very amorous. See l. 46 above: 'ladies' chambers.'

*Ant.* Gentlemen,
We have lost much plate you know; and but this evening
Jewels, to the value of four thousand ducats
Are missing in the duchess' cabinet—
Are the gates shut?

*Off.* Yes.

*Ant.* 'Tis the duchess' pleasure
Each officer be lock'd into his chamber
Till the sun-rising; and to send the keys
Of all their chests, and of their outward doors,
Into her bedchamber:—she is very sick.

*Rod.* At her pleasure.

*Ant.* She entreats you take't not ill: the innocent
Shall be the more approv'd by it.

*Bos.* Gentleman o'th' wood-yard, where's your Switzer now?

*1st. Off.* By this hand, 'twas credibly reported by one o' the black guard. [*Exeunt all except* ANTONIO *and* DELIO.]

*Delio.* How fares it with the duchess?

*Ant.* She's expos'd
Unto the worst of torture, pain, and fear:—
Speak to her all happy comfort.

*Delio.* How I do play the fool with mine own danger!

*Ant.* You are this night, dear friend, to post to Rome;
My life lies in your service.

*Delio.* Do not doubt me—

*Ant.* O, 'tis far from me: and yet fear presents me
Somewhat that looks like danger.

*Delio.* Believe it,
'Tis but the shadow of your fear, no more:
How superstitiously we mind our evils!
The throwing down salt, or crossing of a hare,
Bleeding at nose, the stumbling of a horse,
Or singing of a cricket, are of pow'r
To daunt whole man in us. Sir, fare you well:
I wish you all the joys of a bless'd father;

***64. approv'd:*** rewarded, commended. ***65. Gentlemen... wood-yard:*** Bosola mockingly refers to the 'gentlemen o'th' court' (l. 35) who spread the rumour of the Switzer. ***67. black guard:*** menial.

And, for my faith, lay this unto your breast—
Old friends, like old swords, still are trusted best.

[*Exit.*]

*Enter* CARIOLA.

*Cari.* Sir, you are the happy father of a son—
Your wife commends him to you.

*Ant.* Blessed comfort:
For heaven-sake tend her well; I'll presently
Go set a figure for's nativity. *Exeunt.*

***88. set a figure:*** prepare a horoscope.

## Scene iii

*Enter* BOSOLA [*with a dark lantern*].

*Bos.* Sure I did hear a woman shriek: list, hah?
And the sound came, if I receiv'd it right,
From the duchess' lodgings: there's some stratagem
In the confining all our courtiers
To their several wards: I must have part of it,
My intelligence will freeze else:—list again!
It may be 'twas the melancholy bird,
Best friend of silence and of solitariness,
The owl, that scream'd so:—

*Enter* ANTONIO.

hah? Antonio!

*Ant.* I heard some noise: who's there? what art thou? speak.

*Bos.* Antonio? Put not your face nor body
To such a forc'd expression of fear—
I am Bosola; your friend.

*Ant.* Bosola!—
[*Aside*] This mole does undermine me— [*To him*] heard you not
A noise even now?

*Bos.* From whence?

*Ant.* From the duchess' lodging.

*Bos.* Not I: did you?

*Ant.* I did: or else I dream'd.

*Bos.* Let's walk towards it.

*Ant.* No: it may be 'twas
But the rising of the wind:—

*Bos.* Very likely.
Methinks 'tis very cold, and yet you sweat:
You look wildly.

*Ant.* I have been setting a figure

***20. setting a figure:*** casting a horoscope regarding the stolen jewellery.

For the duchess' jewels:—
*Bos.* Ah: and how falls your question?
Do you find it radical?
*Ant.* What's that to you?
'Tis rather to be question'd what design,
When all men were commanded to their lodgings,
Makes you a night-walker.
*Bos.* In sooth I'll tell you:
Now all the court's asleep, I thought the devil
Had least to do here; I came to say my prayers—
And if it do offend you I do so,
You are a fine courtier.
*Ant.* [*Aside*] This fellow will undo me:—
[*To him*] You gave the duchess apricocks today,
Pray heaven they were not poison'd!
*Bos.* Poison'd ! a Spanish fig
For the imputation.
*Ant.* Traitors are ever confident,
Till they are discover'd:—there were jewels stol'n too—
In my conceit, none are to be suspected
More than yourself.
*Bos.* You are a false steward.
*Ant.* Saucy slave! I'll pull thee up by the roots;—
*Bos.* May be the ruin will crush you to pieces.
*Ant.* You are an impudent snake indeed, sir,
Are you scarce warm, and do you show your sting?

* * *

*Ant.* You libel well, sir.
*Bos.* No sir, copy it out.
And I will set my hand to't.
*Ant.* [*Aside*] My nose bleeds:

***22. radical:*** reliable, going to the root of the matter. ***31. a Spanish fig:*** a vulgar term of contempt accompanied with a rude gesture with the thumb. ***38–40. Ant.:*** Two consecutive speeches prefaced by 'Ant.' in the Quarto suggest that there may have been a missing line spoken by Bosola. ***39. scarce warm:*** just out of hibernation, referring to the snake of the preceding line. ***40. copy it out:*** the supposed libel, and I will sign it.

One that were superstitious would count
This ominous;—when it merely comes by chance.
Two letters, that are wrought here for my name,
Are drown'd in blood!
Mere accident:—[*To him*] for you, sir, I'll take order:
I'th' morn you shall be safe:— [*Aside*] 'tis that must colour
Her lying-in:—[*To him*] sir, this door you pass not:
I do not hold it fit that you come near
The duchess' lodgings, till you have quit yourself.
[*Aside*] *The great are like the base—nay, they are the same—*
*When they seek shameful ways, to avoid shame.* *Exit.*

Bos. Antonio hereabout did drop a paper—
Some of your help, false friend—O, here it is:
What's here? a child's nativity calculated!
[*Reads*] *The duchess was delivered of a son, 'tween the hours twelve and one, in the night: Anno Dom. 1504,*—that's this year—*decimo nono Decembris,*—that's this night—*taken according to the meridian of Malfi*—that's our duchess: happy discovery!—*The lord of the first house, being combust in the ascendant, signifies short life: and Mars being in a human sign, joined to the tail of the Dragon, in the eighth house, doth threaten a violent death; caetera non scrutantur.*
Why now 'tis most apparent: this precise fellow
Is the duchess' bawd:—I have it to my wish;
This is a parcel of intelligency
Our courtiers were cas'd up for!
It needs must follow
That I must be committed on pretence
Of poisoning her; which I'll endure, and laugh at:—
If one could find the father now! But that
Time will discover. Old Castruchio

***44. wrought:*** embroidered initials on the handkerchief that he has taken out to stop the nose-bleed. In the confusion he drops the piece of paper. ***54. false friend:*** the dark lantern. ***56–64. The duchess...scrutantur:*** The technical terms used here indicate Webster's familiarity with astrology. ***65. precise:*** specific. ***66. bawd:*** go-between or pander. Bosola does not suspect Antonio himself to be the father. ***67. parcel:*** item. ***68. cas'd:*** confined.

I'th' morning posts to Rome; by him I'll send
A letter, that shall make her brothers' galls
O'erflow their livers—this was a thrifty way.
Though lust do mask in ne'er so strange disguise,
*She's oft found witty, but is never wise.* [*Exit.*]

## Scene iv

*Enter* CARDINAL *and* JULIA.

*Card.* Sit: thou art my best of wishes—prithee tell me
What trick didst thou invent to come to Rome
Without thy husband.

*Julia.* Why, my lord, I told him
I came to visit an old anchorite
Here, for devotion.

*Card.* Thou art a witty false one:—
I mean to him.

*Julia.* You have prevail'd with me
Beyond my strongest thoughts: I would not now
Find you inconstant.

*Card.* Do not put thyself
To such a voluntary torture, which proceeds
Out of your own guilt.

*Julia.* How, my lord?

*Card.* You fear
My constancy, because you have approv'd
Those giddy and wild turnings in yourself.

*Julia.* Did you e'er find them?

*Card.* Sooth, generally for women:
A man might strive to make glass malleable,
Ere he should make them fixed.

*Julia.* So, my lord—

*Card.* We had need go borrow that fantastic glass
Invented by Galileo the Florentine,
To view another spacious world i'th' moon
And look to find a constant woman there.

*Julia.* This is very well, my lord.

*Card.* Why do you weep?
Are tears your justification? the self-same tears
Will fall into your husband's bosom, lady,

***4. anchorite:*** hermit. ***11. approv'd:*** found. ***17. Galileo:*** The Italian scientist and astronomer (1564–1642) who invented the telescope. ***21. justification:*** defence.

With a loud protestation, that you love him
Above the world:— come, I'll love you wisely,
That's jealously, since I am very certain
You cannot me make cuckold.

*Julia.* I'll go home
To my husband.

*Card.* You may thank me, lady,
I have taken you off your melancholy perch,
Bore you upon my fist, and show'd you game,
And let you fly at it:—I pray thee kiss me—
When thou wast with thy husband, thou wast watch'd
Like a tame elephant:—still you are to thank me—
Thou hadst only kisses from him, and high feeding,
But what delight was that? 'twas just like one
That hath a little fing'ring on the lute,
Yet cannot tune it:—still you are to thank me.

*Julia.* You told me of a piteous wound i'th heart,
And a sick liver, when you woo'd me first,
And spake like one in physic.

*Card.* Who's that?—
Rest firm: for my affection to thee,
Lightning moves slow to't.

*Enter* Servant.

*Serv.* Madam, a gentleman,
That's come post from Malfi, desires to see you.

*Card.* Let him enter, I'll withdraw. *Exit.*

*Serv.* He says,
Your husband, old Castruchio, is come to Rome,
Most pitifully tir'd with riding post. [*Exit.*]

*Enter* DELIO.

*Julia.* [*Aside*] Signior Delio! 'tis one of my old suitors. 46

*Delio.* I was bold to come and see you.

*Julia.* Sir, you are welcome.

***25. jealously:*** or 'earnestly'. There is probably a play on this and the common meaning. ***26. cuckold:*** Since he is not married he cannot be made into a cuckold i.e. a husband whose wife deceives him, often depicted with horns on his head. ***28–9. perch...fist:*** Images taken from falconry. ***38. liver:*** seat of affection. See note on I. i. 303.

*Delio.* Do you lie here?
*Julia.* Sure, your own experience
Will satisfy you, no—our Roman prelates
Do not keep lodging for ladies.
*Delio.* Very well:
I have brought you no commendations from your husband,
For I know none by him.
*Julia.* I hear he's come to Rome?
*Delio.* I never knew man and beast, of a horse and a knight,
So weary of each other—if he had had a good back,
He would have undertook to have borne his horse,
His breech was so pitifully sore.
*Julia.* Your laughter
Is my pity.
*Delio.* Lady, I know not whether
You want money, but I have brought you some.
*Julia.* From my husband?
*Delio.* No, from mine own allowance.
*Julia.* I must hear the condition, ere I be bound to take it.
*Delio.* Look on't, 'tis gold—hath it not a fine colour?
*Julia.* I have a bird more beautiful.
*Delio.* Try the sound on't.
*Julia.* A lute-string far exceeds it;
It hath no smell, like cassia or civet,
Not is it physical, though some fond doctors
Persuade us seethe 't in cullises—I'll tell you,
This is a creature bred by …

[*Enter* Servant.]

*Serv.* Your husband's come,
Hath deliver'd a letter to the Duke of Calabria,
That, to my thinking, hath put him out of his wits. [*Exit.*]
*Julia.* Sir, you hear—
Pray let me know your business and your suit,
As briefly as can be.

***64. cassia:*** a kind of cinnamon. ***64. civet:*** musk, a scent obtained from the civet cat. ***65. physical:*** medicinal. ***65. fond:*** foolish. ***66. cullises:*** medicinal broth.

*Delio.* With good speed—I would wish you
(At such time as you are non-resident
With your husband) my mistress.

*Julia.* Sir, I'll go ask my husband if I shall,
And straight return your answer. *Exit.*

*Delio.* Very fine!
Is this her wit or honesty that speaks thus?
I heard one say the duke was highly mov'd
With a letter sent from Malfi:—I do fear
Antonio is betray'd. How fearfully
Shows his ambition now! unfortunate fortune!
*They pass through whirlpools and deep woes do shun,*
*Who the event weigh, ere the action's done.* *Exit.*

## Scene v

*Enter* Cardinal, *and* FERDINAND *with a letter.*

*Ferd.* I have this night digg'd up a mandrake.
*Card.* Say you?
*Ferd.* And I am grown mad with't.
*Card.* What's the prodigy ?
*Ferd.* Read there—a sister damn'd; she's loose i'th' hilts:
Grown a notorious strumpet.
*Card.* Speak lower.
*Ferd.* Lower?
Rogues do not whisper 't now, but seek to publish't
(As servants do the bounty of their lords)
Aloud; and with a covetous searching eye
To mark who note them:—O confusion seize her!
She hath had most cunning bawds to serve her turn,
And more secure conveyances for lust
Than towns of garrison for service.
*Card.* Is't possible ?
Can this be certain?
*Ferd.* Rhubarb, O for rhubarb
To purge this choler! here's the cursed day
To prompt my memory, and here't shall stick
Till of her bleeding heart I make a sponge
To wipe it out.
*Card.* Why do you make yourself
So wild a tempest?
*Ferd.* Would I could be one,
That I might toss her palace 'bout her ears,

***1. mandrake:*** mandragora, a poisonous plant. According to popular theory it was supposed to shriek when dug up, and anyone who heard it went mad. The implication of madness is ironical. ***3. loose i'th' hilts:*** unchaste. The hilt is the handle of a dagger i.e. loose to the very handle. ***12–13. rhubarb...choler:*** Choler or rage is one of the humours. Rhubarb was considered to be a prescription for excessive rage. ***13. here's...cursed day:*** could be referring to the horoscope which Bosola has sent or to Bosola's letter. ***14. here't:*** The second 'here' could be his own heart which he beats wildly. See next line.

Root up her goodly forests, blast her meads,
And lay her general territory as waste
As she hath done her honours.

*Card.* Shall our blood,
The royal blood of Arragon and Castile,
Be thus attainted?

*Ferd.* Apply desperate physic:
We must not now use balsamum, but fire,
The smarting cupping-glass, for that's the mean
To purge infected blood, such blood as hers:—
There is a kind of pity in mine eye,
I'll give it to my handkercher; and now 'tis here,
I'll bequeath this to her bastard.

*Card.* What to do?

*Ferd.* Why, to make soft lint for his mother's wounds,
When I have hew'd her to pieces.

*Card.* Curs'd creature !
Unequal nature, to place women's hearts
So far upon the left side!

Ferd. Foolish men,
That e'er will trust their honour in a bark
Made of so slight, weak bulrush as is woman,
Apt every minute to sink it!

*Card.* Thus ignorance, when it hath purchas'd honour,
It cannot wield it.

*Ferd.* Methinks I see her laughing—
Excellent hyena!—talk to me somewhat, quickly,
Or my imagination will carry me
To see her, in the shameful act of sin.

*Card.* With whom?

*Ferd.* Happily with some strong thigh'd bargeman;
Or one o'th' wood-yard, that can quoit the sledge,
Or toss the bar, or else some lovely squire
That carries coals up to her privy lodgings.

***21–3. our blood...attainted:*** She has tainted their whole family (blood). Ferdinand in l. 26 speaks specifically of *her* corrupt blood. ***24. balsamum:*** aromatic resin used as balm. ***25. cupping glass:*** a surgical cup used for blood-letting. ***33. the left side:*** the wrong side. ***42. Happily:*** perchance. ***43. o'th' wood-yard:*** See II.ii.65, note. ***43. quoit the sledge:*** throw the sledge hammer, therefore a muscular man. ***45. privy:*** private.

*Card.* You fly beyond your reason.
*Ferd.* Go to, mistress!
'Tis not your whore's milk that shall quench my wild-fire,
But your whore's blood.
*Card.* How idly shows this rage! which carries you,
As men convey'd by witches through the air,
On violent whirlwinds—this intemperate noise
Fitly resembles deaf men's shrill discourse,
Who talk aloud, thinking all other men
To have their imperfection.
*Ferd.* Have not you
My palsy?
*Card.* Yes—I can be angry
Without this rupture: there is not in nature
A thing that makes man so deform'd, so beastly,
As doth intemperate anger:—chide yourself.
You have divers men who never yet express'd
Their strong desire of rest, but by unrest,
By vexing of themselves:—come, put yourself
In tune.
*Ferd.* So; I will only study to seem
The thing I am not. I could kill her now,
In you, or in myself, for I do think
It is some sin in us, heaven doth revenge
By her.
*Card.* Are you stark mad?
*Ferd.* I would have their bodies
Burnt in a coal-pit, with the ventage stopp'd.
That their curs'd smoke might not ascend to heaven:
Or dip the sheets they lie in, in pitch or sulphur,
Wrap them in't, and then light them like a match;
Or else to boil their bastard to a cullis,
And give 't his lecherous father, to renew
The sin of his back.
*Card.* I'll leave you.
*Ferd.* Nay, I have done—

***55. palsy:*** paralysis, paralysed with anger. ***56. rupture:*** breaking out into passion. ***71. cullis:*** See II.iv. 66, note.

I am confident, had I been damn'd in hell
And should have heard of this, it would have put me
Into a cold sweat:—In, in; I'll go sleep—
Till I know who leaps my sister, I'll not stir:
That known, I'll find scorpions to string my whips,
And fix her in a general eclipse. *Exeunt.*

*79.* ***general:*** total.

# ACT III

## Scene i

*Enter* ANTONIO *and* DELIO.

*Ant.* Our noble friend, my most beloved Delio!
O, you have been a stranger long at court—
Came you along with the Lord Ferdinand?
*Delio.* I did sir; and how fares your noble duchess?
*Ant.* Right fortunately well: she's an excellent
Feeder of pedigrees; since you last saw her,
She hath had two children more, a son and daughter.
*Delio.* Methinks 'twas yesterday: let me but wink,
And not behold your face, which to mine eye
Is somewhat leaner, verily I should dream
It were within this half-hour.
*Ant.* You have not been in law, friend Delio,
Nor in prison, nor a suitor at the court,
Nor begg'd the reversion of some great man's place,
Nor troubled with an old wife, which doth make
Your time so insensibly hasten.
*Delio.* Pray sir, tell me,
Hath not his news arriv'd yet to the ear
Of the Lord Cardinal?
*Ant.* I fear it hath—
The Lord Ferdinand, that's newly come to court,
Doth bear himself right dangerously.
*Delio.* Pray why?
*Ant.* He is so quiet, that he seems to sleep
The tempest out, as dormice do in winter:
Those houses that are haunted are most still,
Till the devil be up.

***8. wink:*** close my eyes. ***12–16. You have not… hasten:*** Delio has implied that he cannot believe so much time has elapsed, to which Antonio replies that time drags only with persons like those mentioned in the passage. See comment on Webster's handling of time in *Introduction* pp. xxviii and xxix. ***22. dormice:*** Dormice were supposed to sleep through winter in hibernation.

*Delio.* What say the common people?
*Ant.* The common rabble do directly say
She is a strumpet.
*Delio.* And your graver heads,
Which would be politic, what censure they?
*Ant.* They do observe I grow to infinite purchase
The left-hand way, and all suppose the duchess
Would amend it, if she could: for, say they,
Great princes, though they grudge their officers
Should have such large and unconfined means
To get wealth under them, will not complain
Lest thereby they should make them odious
Unto the people—for other obligation
Of love, or marriage, between her and me,
They never dream of.

*Enter* FERDINAND *and* Duchess.

*Delio.* The Lord Ferdinand
Is going to bed.
*Ferd.* I'll instantly to bed,
For I am weary:- I am to bespeak
A husband for you.
*Duch.* For me, sir! pray who is't?
*Ferd.* The great Count Malateste.
*Duch.* Fie upon him,—
A count! he's a mere stick of sugar-candy,
You may look quite thorough him: when I choose
A husband, I will marry for your honour.
*Ferd.* You shall do well in't:—how is't, worthy Antonio?
*Duch.* But sir, I am to have private conference with you
About a scandalous report, is spread
Touching mine honour.
*Ferd.* Let me be ever deaf to't:
One of Pasquil's paper bullets, court-calumny,

***27. what censure they:*** what judgement do they give? ***28. purchase:*** wealth. ***29. left-hand way:*** dishonestly. ***41. Count Malateste:*** one of the minor characters introduced by Webster and not present in Painter, to widen the court setting. ***49. Pasquil's …bullets:*** Pasquil was reportedly a 15th century schoolmaster or, according to some, a cobbler who lived in Rome. He wrote topical lampoons or pasquinades as they were called after him.

A pestilent air which princes' palaces
Are seldom purg'd of: yet, say that it were true,—
I pour it in your bosom—my fix'd love
Would strongly excuse, extenuate, nay, deny
Faults, were they apparent in you: go be safe
In your own innocency.

*Duch.* O bless'd comfort!
This deadly air is purg'd. *Exeunt* [*all except* FERDINAND].

*Ferd.* Her guilt treads on
Hot-burning coulters:—

*Enter* BOSOLA.

Now Bosola,
How thrives our intelligence?

*Bos.* Sir, uncertainly:
'Tis rumour'd she hath had three bastards, but
By whom, we may go read i'th' stars.

*Ferd.* Why some
Hold opinion, all things are written there.

*Bos.* Yes, if we could find spectacles to read them—
I do suspect there hath been some sorcery
Us'd on the duchess.

*Ferd.* Sorcery! to what purpose?

*Bos.* To make her dote on some desertless fellow
She shames to acknowledge.

*Ferd.* Can your faith give way
To think there's pow'r in potions, or in charms,
To make us love, whether we will or no?

*Bos.* Most certainly.

*Ferd.* Away, these are mere gulleries, horrid things

***51–5. yet...innocency:*** Ferdinand deliberately deludes her into a sense of false security as can be seen in the Duchess's remark that follows. ***57. Hot-burning coulters:*** The ironical reference is to the old tradition that chaste women publicly proved their chastity when accused of its violation by performing the ordeal of fire-walking—walking on red-hot coulters or ploughshares. Camden, in his *Britain* (tr. 1610) refers to Emma, the mother of Edward the Confessor who walked 'barefoot upon nine culters red hote in Winchester Church without harm (an usual kind of triall in those daies and then called Ordalium) and so cleered her selfe of that imputation, that she made her chastitie by so great a miracle more famous to posterity'. ***70. gulleries:*** tricks.

Invented by some cheating mountebanks
To abuse us:—do you think that herbs or charms
Can force the will? Some trials have been made
In this foolish practice; but the ingredients
Were lenitive poisons, such as are of force
To make the patient mad; and straight the witch
Swears, by equivocation, they are in love.
The withcraft lies in her rank blood: this night
I will force confession from her. You told me
You had got, within these two days, a false key
Into her bed-chamber.

*Bos.* I have.

*Ferd.* As I would wish.

*Bos.* What do you intend to do?

*Ferd.* Can you guess?

*Bos.* No:—

*Ferd.* Do not ask then:
He that can compass me, and know my drifts,
May say he hath put a girdle 'bout the world
And sounded all her quicksands.

*Bos.* I do not
Think so.

*Ferd.* What do you think then? pray?

*Bos.* That you
Are your own chronicle too much; and grossly
Flatter yourself.

*Ferd.* Give me thy hand, I thank thee:
I never gave pension but to flatterers,
Till I entertained thee. Farewell:
*That friend a great man's ruin strongly checks*
*Who rails into his belief all his defects.* *Exeunt.*

*71.* ***mountebanks:*** quacks. *73.* ***will:*** here means passion, sexual appetite. *74.* ***but:*** unless if. *75.* ***lenitive poisons:*** soothing to taste, but powerful in effect, driving people crazy. *84–6.* ***He that can…quicksands:*** It is as impossible to understand me and know my thoughts as it is to circumnavigate the world etc. *87–9.* ***That you… flatter yourself:*** You overassess yourself. *90–3.* ***I never…defects:*** Ferdinand appreciates the fact that unlike flatterers, Bosola criticises him.

## Scene ii

*Enter* Duchess, ANTONIO *and* CARIOLA.

*Duch.* Bring me the casket hither, and the glass:—
You get no lodging here tonight, my lord.
*Ant.* Indeed, I must persuade one:—
*Duch.* Very good:
I hope in time 'twill grow into a custom
That noblemen shall come with cap and knee,
To purchase a night's lodging of their wives.
*Ant.* I must lie here.
*Duch.* Must? you are a lord of mis-rule.
*Ant.* Indeed, my rule is only in the night.
*Duch.* To what use will you put me?
*Ant.* We'll sleep together:—
*Duch.* Alas, what pleasure can two lovers find in sleep?
*Cari.* My lord, I lie with her often; and I know
She'll much disquiet you:—
*Ant.* See, you are complain'd of.
*Cari.* For she's the sprawling'st bedfellow.
*Ant.* I shall like her the better for that.
*Cari.* Sir, shall I ask you a question?
*Ant.* I pray thee, Cariola.
*Cari.* Wherefore still when you lie with my lady
Do you rise so early?
*Ant.* Labouring men
Count the clock oft'nest Cariola,
Are glad when their task's ended.
*Duch.* I'll stop your mouth.
[*Kisses him.*]
*Ant.* Nay, that's but one—Venus had two soft doves

***5. with...knee:*** kneeling, with uncovered head—a gesture of humility. ***7. lord of misrule:*** At feasts and revels and particularly at Christmas, a person, usually very young and of inferior social status, was appointed leader, thus turning topsy-turvy (misrule) all traditional norms. ***17. still:*** always. ***18–20. Labouring... ended:*** Antonio is teasing his wife. ***21. Venus:*** Roman goddess of love. Her chariot, according to mythology, was drawn by doves.

To draw her chariot: I must have another. [*Kisses her.*]
When wilt thou marry, Cariola?

*Cari.* Never, my lord.

*Ant.* O fie upon this single life! forgo it!
We read how Daphne, for her peevish flight,
Became a fruitless bay-tree; Syrinx turn'd
To the pale empty reed; Anaxarete
Was frozen into marble: whereas those
Which marry'd, or prov'd kind unto their friends,
Were, by a gracious influence, transshap'd
Into the olive, pomegranate, mulberry;
Became flow'rs, precious stones, or eminent stars.

*Cari.* This is a vain poetry: but I pray you tell me,
If there were propos'd me, wisdom, riches, and beauty,
In three several young men, which should I choose?

*Ant.* 'Tis a hard question: this was Paris' case
And he was blind in't, and there was great cause;
For how was't possible he could judge right,
Having three amorous goddesses in view,
And they stark naked? 'twas a motion
Were able to benight the apprehension
Of the severest counsellor of Europe.
Now I look on both your faces so well form'd,
It puts me in mind of a question I would ask.

*Cari.* What is't?

*Ant.* I do wonder why hard-favour'd ladies,
For the most part, keep worse-favour'd waiting-women
To attend them, and cannot endure fair ones.

***25–32. We read... stars:*** The nymph Daphne, daughter of the Thessalian river-god Peneus, fled from Apollo's embraces and in answer to a prayer, was changed to a bay tree. Similarly Syrinx, when pursued by Pan, the god of shepherds, jumped into a river and was metamorphosed into a reed. Venus punished the heartless Anaxarete for whom her rejected lover hanged himself at her door by turning her into a stone. Antonio deliberately misinterprets the myths by drawing the conclusion that women who wish to remain single are metamorphosed into sterile objects. There are, however, no well-known myths about the olive, pomegranate and mulberry. ***36. Paris.*** Paris, the son of Priam, King of Troy. The Greek myth recounts how the three goddesses Hera, Aphrodite and Athene tossed a golden apple to earth and asked Paris to give it to the most beautiful of the three. Paris gave it to Aphrodite, the goddess of love, who rewarded him by giving him Helen, the wife of King Menelaus of Greece. This started the Trojan War that is the subject of Homer's epic, *The Iliad.*

*Duch.* O, that's soon answer'd.
Did you ever in your life know an ill painter
Desire to have his dwelling next door to the shop
Of an excellent picture-maker? 'twould disgrace
His face-making, and undo him:—I prithee,
When were we so merry?—my hair tangles.

*Ant.* Pray thee, Cariola, let's steal forth the room
And let her talk to herself; I have divers times
Serv'd her the like, when she hath chaf'd extremely:
I love to see her angry:—softly, Cariola.
*Exit with* CARIOLA.

*Duch.* Doth not the colour of my hair 'gin to change?
When I wax gray, I shall have all the court
Powder their hair with arras, to be like me:—
You have cause to love me; I enter'd you into my heart
Before you would vouchsafe to call for the keys.

*Enter* FERDINAND [*behind*].

We shall one day have my brothers take you napping:
Methinks his presence, being now in court,
Should make you keep your own bed: but you'll say
Love mix'd with fear is sweetest. I'll assure you
You shall get no more children till my brothers
Consent to be your gossips:— have you lost your tongue?
[*Turns and sees Ferdinand.*]
'Tis welcome:
For know, whether I am doom'd to live or die,
I can do both like a prince.
*Ferdinand gives her a poniard.*

*Ferd.* Die then, quickly!
Virtue, where art thou hid? what hideous thing
Is it that doth eclipse thee?

*Duch.* Pray sir, hear me:—

***60. arras:*** a white powder derived from the orris-root. ***62. keys:*** of her heart. ***63. We shall... napping:*** There is superb irony as she says this, without knowing that Ferdinand is behind her. The whole passage is very dramatic, contrasting the light badinage that precedes to the horror that immediately follows. ***68. gossips:*** The original meaning of the O.E word 'god-sibb' was 'god-parent'. ***72–85. Virtue... flown:*** The entire passage contains echoes from Sidney's *Arcadia*.

*Ferd.* Or is it true, thou art but a bare name,
And no essential thing?
*Duch.* Sir:—
*Ferd.* Do not speak.
*Duch.* No sir:
I will plant my soul in mine ears to hear you.
*Ferd.* O most imperfect light of human reason,
That mak'st us so unhappy, to foresee
What we can least prevent! Pursue thy wishes,
And glory in them: there's in shame no comfort
But to be past all bounds, and sense of shame.
*Duch.* I pray sir, hear me: I am married.
*Feed.* So:—
*Duch.* Happily, not to your liking: but for that,
Alas, your shears do come untimely now
To clip the bird's wings that's already flown!
Will you see my husband?
*Ferd.* Yes, if I could change
Eyes with a basilisk:—
*Duch.* Sure, you came hither
By his confederacy.
*Ferd.* The howling of a wolf
Is music to thee, screech-owl, prithee peace!
Whate'er thou art, that hast enjoy'd my sister,—
For I am sure thou hear'st me—for thine own sake
Let me not know thee: I came hither prepar'd
To work thy discovery, yet am now persuaded
It would beget such violent effects
As would damn us both:—I would not for ten millions
I had beheld thee; therefore use all means
I never may have knowledge of thy name;
Enjoy thy lust still, and a wretched life,
On that condition.—And for thee, vile woman,
If thou do wish thy lecher may grow old
In thy embracements, I would have thee build

*83. **Happily:*** perhaps. *87. **basilisk:*** a mythical serpent that killed or turned to stone all it looked at. Also called a *cockatrice* as in *Rom. and Jul*. (III. ii. 47): 'The death-darling eye of cockatrice'. *88. **howling of a wolf:*** (Irony) In Act V Ferdinand is afflicted by lycanthropia, and he imagines he is a wolf. *89. **to thee:*** compared to thee.

Such a room for him as our anchorites
To holier use inhabit: let not the sun
Shine on him, till he's dead; let dogs and monkeys
Only converse with him, and such dumb things
To whom nature denies use to sound his name;
Do not keep a paraquito, lest she learn it.
If thou do love him, cut out thine own tongue
Lest it bewray him.

*Duch.* Why might not I marry?
I have not gone about, in this, to create
Any new world, or custom.

*Ferd.* Thou art undone:
And thou hast ta'en that massy sheet of lead
That hid thy husband's bones, and folded it
About my heart.

*Duch.* Mine bleeds for't.

*Ferd.* Thine? thy heart?
What should I name't, unless a hollow bullet
Fill'd with unquenchable wild-fire?

*Duch.* You are, in this,
Too strict: and were you not my princely brother
I would say too wilful: my reputation
Is safe.

*Ferd.* Dost thou know what reputation is?
I'll tell thee—to small purpose, since th'instruction
Comes now too late:
Upon a time, Reputation, Love, and Death
Would travel o'er the world; and it was concluded
That they should part, and take three several ways:
Death told them, they should find him in great battles,
Or cities plagu'd with plagues; Love gives them counsel
To inquire for him 'mongst unambitious shepherds,
Where dowries were not talk'd of, and sometimes
'Mongst quiet kindred that had nothing left

*122–35. Upon a time...invisible:* This long fable from Ferdinand may seem inappropriate in this emotionally-charged scene, as may the Duchess's tale of the salmon and the dog-fish at the end of Act III, sc. v, but in both scenes it is psychologically plausible that they are distancing or distracting the mind from the immediacy of the moment to control their emotions.

By their dead parents: 'Stay', quoth Reputation,
'Do not forsake me; for it is my nature
If once I part from any man I meet
I am never found again.' And so, for you:
You have shook hands with Reputation,
And made him invisible:—so fare you well.
I will never see you more.

*Duch.* Why should only I,
Of all the other princes of the world,
Be cas'd up, like a holy relic? I have youth,
And a little beauty.

*Ferd.* So you have some virgins
That are witches:—I will never see thee more. *Exit.*

*Enter* ANTONIO *with a pistol* [, *and* CARIOLA].

*Duch.* You saw this apparition?

*Ant.* Yes: we are
Betray'd; how came he hither? I should turn
This to thee, for that.

*Cari.* Pray sir, do: and when
That you have cleft my heart, you shall read there
Mine innocence.

*Duch.* That gallery gave him entrance.

*Ant.* I would this terrible thing would come again,
That, standing on my guard, I might relate
My warrantable love:— *She shews the poniard.*
ha, what means this?

*Duch.* He left this with me:—

*Ant.* And it seems did wish
You would use it on yourself?

*Duch.* His action seem'd
To intend so much.

*Ant.* This hath a handle to't
As well as a point—turn it towards him,
And so fasten the keen edge in his rank gall:—
[*Knocking within.*]
How now! who knocks? more earthquakes?

***135. invisible:*** lost him for ever. ***144. this:*** the pistol. He suspects Cariola of betraying.

*Duch.* I stand
As if a mine, beneath my feet, were ready
To be blown up.

*Cari.* 'Tis Bosola:—

*Duch.* Away!
O misery! methinks unjust actions
Should wear these masks and curtains, and not we:—
You must instantly part hence; I have fashion'd it already.
*Exit* ANTONIO.

*Enter* BOSOLA.

*Bos.* The duke your brother is ta'en up in a whirlwind,
Hath took horse, and's rid post to Rome.

*Duch.* So late?

*Bos.* He told me, as he mounted into th' saddle,
You were undone.

*Duch.* Indeed, I am very near it.

*Bos.* What's the matter?

*Duch.* Antonio, the master of our household,
Hath dealt so falsely with me, in's accounts:
My brother stood engag'd with me for money
Ta'en up of certain Neapolitan Jews,
And Antonio lets the bonds be forfeit.

*Bos.* Strange!—[*Aside*] This is cunning:—

*Duch.* And hereupon
My brother's bills at Naples are protested
Against:—call up our officers.

*Bos.* I shall. *Exit.*

[*Enter* ANTONIO.]

*Duch.* The place that you must fly to is Ancona,
Hire a house there. I'll send after you
My treasure and my jewels: our weak safety
Runs upon enginous wheels; short syllables

***158. unjust:*** wrong; evil. ***160. fashion'd it:*** worked out my plan of action. The Duchess is a quick thinker in times of crisis, and unlike Antonio does not lose her head. In ll.166–70 and ll.174–6 we see her plan of action. ***166–70. Antonio… forfeit:*** The Duchess pretends that Antonio has allowed the bonds to lapse and Ferdinand's bills of exchange (l.172) are not being accepted in Naples. ***177. enginous wheels:*** fast movement or devious methods. 'Enginous' could also mean 'ingenious'.

Must stand for periods. I must now accuse you
Of such a feigned crime as Tasso calls
*Magnanima menzogna:* a noble lie
'Cause it must shield our honours:—hark! they are coming.

*Enter* [BOSOLA *and*] Officers.

*Ant.* Will your grace hear me?
*Duch.* I have got well by you: you have yielded me
A million of loss; I am like to inherit
The people's curses for your stewardship.
You had the trick in audit-time to be sick,
Till I had sign'd your *quietus*; and that cur'd you
Without help of a doctor.—Gentlemen,
I would have this man be an example to you all:
So shall you hold my favour; I pray let him,
For h'as done that, alas, you would not think of,
And, because I intend to be rid of him,
I mean not to publish:—use your fortune elsewhere.
*Ant.* I am strongly arm'd to brook my overthrow,
As commonly men bear with a hard year:
I will not blame the cause on't; but do think
The necessity of my malevolent star
Procures this, not her humour. O the inconstant
And rotten ground of service!—you may see:
'Tis ev'n like him, that in a winter night
Takes a long slumber o'er a dying fire,
As loth to part from't; yet parts thence as cold
As when he first sat down.
*Duch.* We do confiscate,
Towards the satisfying of your accounts,
All that you have.
*Ant.* I am all yours: and 'tis very fit
All mine should be so.
*Duch.* So, sir; you have your pass.
*Ant.* You may see, gentlemen, what'tis to serve
A prince with body, and soul. *Exit.*

***180. Magnanima menzogna:*** noble lie. ***187. quietus:*** had you discharged. See I. i. 469 note. ***187. cur'd:*** saved. ***206–7. I am all... be so:*** double meaning.

*Bos.* Here's an example, for extortion:
what moisture is drawn out of the sea, when foul weather comes, pours
down and runs into the sea again.

*Duch.* I would know what are your opinions of this Antonio.

*2nd. Off.* He could not abide to see a pig's head gaping:
I thought your grace would find him a Jew.

*3rd. Off.* I would you had been his officer, for your own sake.

*4th. Off.* You would have had more money.

*1st. Off.* He stopp'd his ears with black wool; and to those came to him for money, said he was thick of hearing.

*2nd. Off.* Some said he was an hermaphrodite, for he could not abide a woman.

*4th. Off.* How scurvy proud he would look, when the treasury was full! Well, let him go:—

*1st. Off.* Yes, and the chippings of the buttery fly after him,
to scour his gold chain.

*Duch.* Leave us. *Exeunt* Officers.
What do you think of these?

*Bos.* That these are rogues, that in's prosperity,
But to have waited on his fortune, could have wish'd
His dirty stirrup riveted through their noses,
And follow'd after's mule, like a bear in a ring;
Would have prostituted their daughters to his lust;
Made their first-born intelligencers; thought none happy
But such as were born under his bless'd planet,
And wore his livery: and do these lice drop off now?
Well, never look to have the like again:
He hath left a sort of flatt'ring rogues behind him—
Their doom must follow: princes pay flatterers
In their own money; flatterers dissemble their vices

***210. extortion:*** confiscation of Antonio's wealth. ***214–15. He could not... Jew:*** He is as avaricious as a Jew, and like a Jew he cannot abide pork. ***218. black wool:*** black wool, dipped in certain unguents, was supposed to cure deafness. He had sharp ears but pretended to be deaf as and when it suited him. ***220. hermaphrodite:*** a person possessing properties of both sexes. ***224–5. chippings... chain:*** crumbs picked up (stolen) from the buttery were used to rub his gold chain and make it bright. The gold chain was the steward's badge of office. Cf. *T.N* (II.iii.118–19) where Sir Toby tells Malvolio, 'Go sir, rub your chain with crumbs.' ***231. bear in a ring:*** bear led with a ring through his nose.

And they dissemble their lies: that's justice—
Alas, poor gentleman!
*Duch.* Poor? he hath amply fill'd his coffers.
*Bos.* Sure
He was too honest: Pluto, the god of riches,
When he's sent by Jupiter to any man
He goes limping, to signify that wealth
That comes on god's name comes slowly:
but when he's sent
On the devil's errand, he rides post and
comes in by scuttles.
Let me show you what a most unvalu'd jewel
You have, in a wanton humour, thrown away,
To bless the man shall find him: he was an excellent
Courtier, and most faithful, a soldier that thought it
As beastly to know his own value too little
As devilish to acknowledge it too much:
Both his virtue and form deserv'd a far better fortune.
His discourse rather delighted to judge itself,
than show itself.
His breast was fill'd with all perfection,
And yet it seem'd a private whisp'ring-room,
It made so little noise of 't.
*Duch.* But he was basely descended.
*Bos.* Will you make yourself a mercenary herald,
Rather to examine men's pedigrees than virtues?
You shall want him,
For know an honest statesman to a prince
Is like a cedar, planted by a spring:
The spring bathes the tree's root, the grateful tree
Rewards it with his shadow: you have not done so—
I would sooner swim to the Bermudas on
Two politicians' rotten bladders, tied
Together with an intelligencer's heart-string,

***243. Pluto:*** the god of the underworld often mistakenly identified with Plutus, the god of wealth. ***247. scuttles:*** runs, hastens. ***248. unvalued:*** priceless. ***259. herald:*** officer at ceremonial royal occasions who recorded names and pedigrees of all entrants. ***266. Bermudas:*** In May 1609, a fleet of nine ships under Sir Thomas Gates and Sir George Summers set sail for Virginia. But the *Sea-Adventurer* carrying Gates and

Than depend on so changeable a prince's favour.
Fare thee well, Antonio; since the malice of the world
Would needs down with thee; it cannot be said yet
That any ill happened unto thee,
Considering thy fall was accompanied with virtue.

*Duch.* O, you render me excellent music.

*Bos.* Say you?

*Duch.* This good one that you speak of, is my husband.

*Bos.* Do I not dream? can this ambitious age
Have so much goodness in't, as to prefer
A man merely for worth, without these shadows
Of wealth, and painted honours? possible?

*Duch.* I have had three children by him.

*Bos.* Fortunate lady!
For you have made your private nuptial bed
The humble and fair seminary of peace:
No question but many an unbenefic'd scholar
Shall pray for you for this deed, and rejoice
That some preferment in the world can yet
Arise from merit. The virgins of your land
That have no dowries, shall hope your example
Will raise them to rich husbands: should you want
Soldiers, 'twould make the very Turks and Moors
Turn Christians, and serve you for this act.
Last, the neglected poets of your time,
In honour of this trophy of a man,
Rais'd by that curious engine, your white hand,
Shall thank you, in your grave, for't; and make that
More reverend than all the cabinets
Of living princes. For Antonio,
His fame shall likewise flow from many a pen,
When heralds shall want coats to sell to men.

*Duch.* As I taste comfort in this friendly speech,

Summers got separated from the rest of the fleet by a storm, though eventually the entire crew survived. The news of the storm reached England by the end of the year and created a great stir. A number of narrative accounts of the shipwreck, subsequently referred to as the Bermuda pamphlets, were published. ***279. painted:*** false. ***282. seminary***: nursery, seed-bed. ***283. unbenefic'd:*** not given a Church benefice or office, and therefore unappreciated. ***298. coats:*** coats of arms to indicate pedigree.

So would I find concealment.

*Bos.* O, the secret of my prince,
Which I will wear on th' inside of my heart.

*Duch.* You shall take charge of all my coin and jewels,
And follow him; for he retires himself
To Ancona.

*Bos.* So.

*Duch.* Whither, within few days,
I mean to follow thee.

*Bos.* Let me think:
I would wish your grace to feign a pilgrimage
To our Lady of Loretto, scarce seven leagues
From fair Ancona; so may you depart
Your country with more honour, and your flight
Will seem a princely progress, retaining
Your usual train about you.

*Duch.* Sir, your direction
Shall lead me by the hand.

*Cari.* In my opinion,
She were better progress to the baths
At Lucca, or go visit the Spa
In Germany, for, if you will believe me,
I do not like this jesting with religion,
This feigned pilgrimage.

*Duch.* Thou art a superstitious fool—
Prepare us instantly for our departure:
Past sorrows, let us moderately lament them,
For those to come, seek wisely to prevent them.
*Exit* [*with* CARIOLA].

*Bos.* A politician is the devil's quilted anvil—
He fashions all sins on him, and the blows
Are never heard: he may work in a lady's chamber,

***307. feign a pilgrimage:*** In Painter's *The Palace of Pleasure* it is the Duchess's gentlewoman who suggests this. Webster attributes the suggestion to Bosola who, perhaps, wants to damn her further for 'jesting with religion'. (l. 317). ***315. Spa***: A spa is any place having a mineral spring with medicinal properties, as in Bath. There was a famous spa in Belgium which was named Spa. Webster may have been confused about its location, but Belgians were often loosely called Germans. ***323. quilted:*** with soft paddings so that the sound is muffled.

As here for proof. What rests, but I reveal
All to my lord? O, this base quality
Of intelligencer! why, every quality i'th' world
Prefers but gain or commendation:
Now, for this act I am certain to be rais'd,
*And men that paint weeds to the life are prais'd.* *Exit.*

***329. prefers:*** begets. ***331. And men…prais'd***: even men who paint worthless things can gain something.

## Scene iii

*Enter* Cardinal *with* MALATESTE, FERDINAND *with* DELIO *and* SILVIO, *and* PESCARA.

*Card.* Must we turn soldier then?

*Mal.* The Emperor,
Hearing your worth that way, ere you attain'd
This reverend garment, joins you in commission
With the right fortunate soldier, the Marquis of Pescara,
And the famous Lannoy.

*Card.* He that had the honour
Of taking the French king prisoner?

*Mal.* The same—
Here's a plot drawn for a new fortification
At Naples. [*They talk apart.*]

*Ferd.* This great Count Malateste, I perceive,
Hath got employment?

*Delio.* No employment, my lord;
A marginal note in the muster-book, that he is
A voluntary lord.

*Ferd.* He's no soldier?

*Delio.* He has worn gunpowder in's hollow tooth,
For the toothache.

*Sil.* He comes to the leaguer with a full intent
To eat fresh beef and garlic, means to stay
Till the scent be gone, and straight return to court.

*Delio.* He hath read all the late service
As the City Chronicle relates it,
And keeps two painters going, only to express
Battles in model.

*Sil.* Then he'll fight by the book.

*1. The Emperor:* probably Charles V. *4. The Marquis of Pescara:* There was a historical Marquis of Pescara who fought in the battle of Pavia in 1525. The action of this play, however, is set around 1504. (See II.iii.58.) *5. Lannoy:* Francis I of France was defeated by Lannoy in 1525 in the battle of Pavia. *7. plot:* plan. *9. Malateste:* See III. i. 41 note. *15. leaguer:* military camp. *21. model:* drawn to scale. *21. by the book:* theoretically.

*Delio.* By the almanac, I think—
To choose good days, and shun the critical.
That's his mistress' scarf.

*Sil.* Yes, he protests
He would do much for that taffeta—

*Delio.* I think he would run away from a battle
To save it from taking prisoner.

*Sil.* He is horribly afraid
Gunpowder will spoil the perfume on't—

*Delio.* I saw a Dutchman break his pate once
For calling him pot-gun; he made his head
Have a bore in't, like a musket.

*Sil.* I would he had made a touch-hole to't.
He is indeed a guarded sumpter-cloth,
Only for the remove of the court.

*Enter* BOSOLA.

*Pes.* Bosola arriv'd! what should be the business?
Some falling out amongst the cardinals.
These factions amongst great men, they are like
Foxes: when their heads are divided
They carry fire in their tails, and all the country
About them goes to wreck for't. [*Ferdinand, Cardinal and Bosola talk apart.*]

*Sil.* What's that Bosola?

*Delio.* I knew him in Padua—a fantastical scholar, like such who study to know how many knots was in Hercules' club, of what colour Achilles' beard was, or whether Hector were not troubled with the toothache; he hath

***24. his mistress's scarf:*** a token of his mistress that a knight-errant used to carry in the Middle Ages, but much ridiculed later (Cf. *Don Quixote*). ***30. pot-gun:*** a wooden toy-gun for children, also a term for a braggart. ***33. guarded sumpter-cloth:*** ornamental saddle-cloth. ***34. remove of the court:*** for ceremonial occasions. ***38–40. Foxes… wreck for't:*** an allusion to Samson (*Judges*, xv, 4–5) who took three hundred foxes and tying them tail to tail put firebrands in the midst between two tails. He then set them loose into the standing corn of the Philistines and so destroyed their harvest. ***41. Padua:*** a famous university where Bosola had studied. Bacon has commented on the Padua type of 'speculative' learning. Padua was founded in 1238. ***42. Hercules:*** most popular of Greek heroes, famous for his strength and courage. ***43. Achilles:*** Greek hero of the Trojan War and leader of the Myrmidons. ***44. Hector:*** eldest son of King Priam of Troy and the bravest of the Trojans.

studied himself half blear-eyed to know the true symmetry of Caesar's nose by a shoeing-horn; and this he did to gain the name of a speculative man.

*Pes.* Mark Prince Ferdinand:
A very salamander lives in's eye,
To mock the eager violence of fire.

*Sil.* That cardinal hath made more bad faces with his oppression than ever Michael Angelo made good ones; he lifts up's nose, like a foul porpoise before a storm—

*Pes.* The Lord Ferdinand laughs.

*Delio.* Like a deadly cannon
That lightens ere it smokes.

*Pes.* These are your true pangs of death,
The pangs of life that struggle with great statesmen—

*Delio.* In such a deformed silence, witches whisper
Their charms.

*Card.* Doth she make religion her riding-hood
To keep her from the sun and tempest?

*Ferd.* That!
That damns her:—methinks her fault and beauty,
Blended together, show like leprosy,
The whiter, the fouler:—I make it a question
Whether her beggarly brats were ever christen'd.

*Card.* I will instantly solicit the state of Ancona
To have them banish'd.

*Ferd.* You are for Loretto?
I shall not be at your ceremony: fare you well—
Write to the Duke of Malfi, my young nephew
She had by her first husband, and acquaint him
With's mother's honesty.

***47. speculative man:*** philosopher. ***49. salamander:*** tailed amphibian, in appearance like a lizard, fabled to live in fire. ***51. bad faces:*** probably they grimace with anger at Bosola's news. ***52. Michael Angelo:*** Italian painter and sculptor of the Renaissance. ***68. your ceremony:*** the formal ceremony of surrendering his religious office and taking on the arms of the soldier. ***69. Duke... nephew:*** the only reference to this son and perhaps a lapse on Webster's part. It is Antonio's son who is established in his mother's right at the end of the play. If 'his mother's right' means the Duchess's paternal wealth, then since the Cardinal and Ferdinand are dead at the end of the play, everything goes to the Duchess and is therefore inherited by Antonio's son.

*Bos.* I will.
*Ferd.* Antonio!
A slave, that only smell'd of ink and counters,
And ne'er in's life look'd like a gentleman,
But in the audit-time—go, go presently,
Draw me out an hundred and fifty of our horse,
And meet me at the fort-bridge, *Exeunt.*

## Scene iv.

*Enter* Two Pilgrims *to the Shrine of our Lady of Loretto.*

*1st. Pil.* I have not seen a goodlier shrine than this,
Yet I have visited many.

*2nd. Pil.* The Cardinal of Arragon
Is this day to resign his cardinal's hat;
His sister duchess likewise is arriv'd
To pay her vow of pilgrimage—I expect
A noble ceremony.

*1st. Pil.* No question:—they come.

*Here the ceremony of the* Cardinal's *instalment in the habit of a soldier, performed in delivering up his cross, hat, robes and ring at the shrine, and investing him with sword, helmet, shield and spurs; then* ANTONIO, *the* Duchess *and their* Children, *having presented themselves at the shrine, are (by a form of banishment in dumb-show expressed towards them by the cardinal and the state of Ancona) banished: during all which ceremony, this ditty is sung, to very solemn music, by divers* Churchmen; *and then exeunt [all, except the* Two Pilgrims].

*Arms and honours deck thy story*
*To thy fame's eternal glory!*
*Adverse fortune ever fly thee,*
*No disastrous fate come nigh thee!*

The author disclaims this ditty to be his.

The dumb show after l.7 is an instance of the more elaborate stage-presentation in Jacobean drama. Webster uses this device in *The White Devil* (Act.II, sc.iii) when Isabella goes up to the poisoned painting of Brachiano and kisses it thrice. This short scene of 75 lines serves a number of functions. It tells us of the Cardinal's preparations for a military expedition and provides the important information that Antonio, the Duchess and their children are banished by the Cardinal from the state of Ancona. This scene also indicates, like a choric comment, the attitude of contemporary bystanders and onlookers. While they are shocked by the excessive cruelty and violence of the Cardinal and while they are sorry for Antonio, they express disapproval of the socially ill-matched marriage of the Duchess with Antonio. Perhaps also there is an ironical implication that religion can offer no sanctuary in this corrupt and vicious world.
***8–23. Arms... show'rs:*** The Quarto edition of 1623 has the marginal note, 'the author disclaims this ditty to be his' beside it.

*I alone will sing thy praises,*
*Whom to honour virtue raises,*
*And thy study, that divine is,*
*Bent to martial discipline is:*
*Lay aside all those robes lie by thee;*
*Crown thy arts with arms, they'll beautify thee.*
*O worthy of worthiest name, adorn'd in this manner,*
*Lead bravely thy forces on under war's warlike banner!*
*O, mayst thou prove fortunate in all martial courses!*
*Guide thou still, by skill, in arts and forces!*
*Victory attend thee nigh whilst Fame sings loud thy pow'rs;*
*Triumphant conquest crown thy head, and blessings pour down show'rs!*

*$1^{st}$. Pil.* Here's a strange turn of state! who would have thought
So great a lady would have match'd herself
Unto so mean a person? yet the cardinal
Bears himself much too cruel.

*$2^{nd}$. Pil.* They are banish'd.

*$1^{st}$. Pil.* But I would ask what power hath this state
Of Ancona to determine of a free prince?

*$2^{nd}$. Pil.* They are a free state sir, and her brother show'd
How that the Pope, fore-hearing of her looseness,
Hath seiz'd into th' protection of the church
The dukedom, which she held as dowager.

*$1^{st}$. Pil.* But by what justice?

*$2^{nd}$. Pil.* Sure, I think by none,
Only her brother's instigation.

*$1^{st}$. Pil.* What was it with such violence he took
Off from her finger?

*$2^{nd}$. Pil.* 'Twas her wedding ring,
Which he vow'd shortly he would sacrifice
To his revenge.

*$1^{st}$. Pil.* Alas, Antonio!
If that a man be thrust into a well,
No matter who sets hand to't, his own weight
Will bring him sooner to th'bottom:—come, let's hence.
Fortune makes this conclusion general:
*All things do help th' unhappy man to fall.* *Exeunt.*

***29. determine:*** take a decision.

## Scene v

*Enter* ANTONIO, Duchess, Children, CARIOLA, Servants.

*Duch.* Banish'd Ancona!
*Ant.* Yes, you see what pow'r
Lightens in great men's breath.
*Duch.* Is all our train
Shrunk to this poor remainder?
*Ant.* These poor men,
Which have got little in your service, vow
To take your fortune: but your wiser buntings,
Now they are fledg'd; are gone.
*Duch.* They have done wisely—
This puts me in mind of death: physicians thus,
With their hands full of money, use to give o'er
Their patients.
*Ant.* Right the fashion of the world:
From decay'd fortunes every flatterer shrinks;
Men cease to build where the foundation sinks.
*Duch.* I had a very strange dream tonight.
*Ant.* What was't?
*Duch.* Methought I wore my coronet of state,
And on a sudden all the diamonds
Were chang'd to pearls.
*Ant.* My interpretation
Is, you'll weep shortly, for to me, the pearls
Do signify your tears:—
*Duch.* The birds that live i' th' field
On the wild benefit of nature, live
Happier than we; for they may choose their mates,
And carol their sweet pleasures to the spring:—

*Enter* BOSOLA [*with a letter*].

**2. lightens:** breathes fire. Cf.III.iii.55. ***5. buntings:*** small birds. ***8–9. With their hands... patients:*** having extorted money from their parents, discard them. ***9. Right:*** exactly. ***18. The birds:*** From now on, bird imagery is frequently used in relation to the Duchess.

*Bos.* You are happily o'erta'en.
*Duch.* From my brother?
*Bos.* Yes, from the Lord Ferdinand, your brother,
All love and safety—
*Duch.* Thou dost blanch mischief,
Wouldst make it white:—see, see, like to calm weather
At sea, before a tempest, false hearts speak fair
To those they intend most mischief.
(Reads) *Send Antonio to me; I want his head in a business:*—
A politic equivocation!
He doth not want your counsel, but your head;
That is, he cannot sleep till you be dead.
And here's another pitfall, that's strew'd o'er
With roses; mark it, 'tis a cunning one:
[Reads] *I stand engaged for your husband, for several debts at Naples: let not that trouble him, I had rather have his heart than his money.*
And I believe so too.
*Bos.* What do you believe?
*Duch.* That he so much distrusts my husband's love,
He will by no means believe his heart is with him
Until he see it: the devil is not cunning enough
To circumvent us in riddles.
*Bos.* Will you reject that noble and free league
Of amity and love which I present you?
*Duch.* Their league is like that of some politic kings,
Only to make themselves of strength and pow'r
To be our after-ruin: tell them so.
*Bos.* And what from you?
*Ant.* Thus tell him: I will not come.
*Bos.* And what of this?
*Ant.* My brothers have dispers'd
Bloodhounds abroad; which till I hear are muzzled,
No truce, though hatch'd with ne'er such politic skill
Is safe, that hangs upon our enemies' will.
I'll not come at them.
*Bos.* This proclaims your breeding.

***24. blanch:*** whitewash. ***42. league:*** gesture of agreement. ***48. this:*** this letter.

Every small thing draws a base mind to fear,
As the adamant draws iron; fare you well sir,
You shall shortly hear from's. *Exit.*

*Duch.* I suspect some ambush:
Therefore by all my love, I do conjure you
To take your eldest son, and fly towards Milan:
Let us not venture all this poor remainder
In one unlucky bottom.

*Ant.* You counsel safely:—
Best of my life, farewell: since we must part
Heaven hath a hand in't; but no otherwise
Than as some curious artist takes in sunder
A clock or watch when it is out of frame,
To bring't in better order.

*Duch.* I know not which is best,
To see you dead, or part with you:—farewell boy;
Thou art happy, that thou hast not understanding
To know thy misery, for all our wit
And reading brings us to a truer sense
Of sorrow:—in the eternal church, sir,
I do hope we shall not part thus.

*Ant.* O, be of comfort!
Make patience a noble fortitude,
And think not how unkindly we are us'd:
*Man, like to cassia, is prov'd best, being bruis'd.*

*Duch.* Must I, like to a slave-born Russian,
Account it praise to suffer tyranny?
And yet, O Heaven, thy heavy hand is in't.
I have seen my little boy oft scourge his top
And compar'd myself to't: naught made me e'er
Go right but heaven's scourge-stick.

*Ant.* Do not weep:
Heaven fashion'd us of nothing; and we strive

***54. adamant:*** magnet or loadstone. ***59–60. venture... bottom:*** a proverb. 'Bottom' is 'ship'. ***71. eternal church:*** a contrast to the church temporal represented by the cruel and corrupt Cardinal. ***73–7. Make patience... tyranny:*** Contrast Antonio's passive acceptance with the Duchess's rebellious pride. ***75. Man... bruis'd:*** Cf. *The White Devil*, I.i.47–8: 'Perfumes, the more they are chafed, the more they render/Their pleasing scents.' ***81. scourge-stick:*** whip.

To bring ourselves to nothing:—farewell Cariola,
And thy sweet armful: if I do never see thee more;
Be a good mother to your little ones,
And save them from the tiger: fare you well.

*Duch.* Let me look upon you once more; for that speech
Came from a dying father: your kiss is colder
Than that I have seen an holy anchorite
Give to a dead man's skull.

*Ant.* My heart is turn'd to a heavy lump of lead,
With which I sound my danger: fare you well.

*Exit [with his elder* Son]

*Duch.* My laurel is all withered.

*Cari.* Look, madam, what a troop of armed men
Make toward us.

*Enter* BOSOLA *with a* Guard, *with visards.*

*Duch.* O, they are very welcome:
When Fortune's wheel is overcharg'd with princes,
The weight makes it move swift. I would have my ruin
Be sudden:—I am your adventure, am I not?

*Bos.* You are, you must see your husband no more—

*Duch.* What devil art thou, that counterfeits heaven's thunder?

*Bos.* Is that terrible? I would have you tell me
Whether is that note worse that frights the silly birds
Out of the corn, or that which doth allure them
To the nets? you have hearken'd to the last too much.

*Duch.* O misery! like to a rusty o'ercharg'd cannon,
Shall I never fly in pieces? come: to what prison?

*Bos.* To none:—

*Duch.* Whither then?

*Bos.* To your palace.

*Duch.* I have heard
That Charon's boat serves to convey all o'er

***93. My laurel… withered:*** Compare Cleopatra on the death of Antony in *Antony and Cleopatra*, IV. xv.64: 'O wither'd is the garland of the war'. ***106. fly in pieces:*** disintegrate into bits. ***108. Charon's boat:*** In Greek mythology, five rivers separated Hades (the underworld) from the land of the living: Styx (hateful), Lethe (forgetfulness), Acheron (woeful), Phlegethon (fiery) and Cocytus (wailing). Charon was the ferryman who ferried the newly-arrived dead across Styx.

The dismal lake, but brings none back again.
*Bos.* Your brothers mean you safety, and pity.
*Duch.* Pity!
With such a pity men preserve alive
Pheasants and quails, when they are not fat enough
To be eaten.
*Bos.* These are your children?
*Dutch.* Yes:—
*Bos.* Can they prattle?
*Duch.* No:
But I intend, since they were born accurs'd,
Curses shall be their first language.
*Bos.* Fie, madam,
Forget this base, low fellow.
*Duch.* Were I a man
I'd beat that counterfeit face into thy other.
*Bos.* One of no birth—
*Duch.* Say that he was born mean:
Man is most happy when's own actions
Be arguments and examples of his virtue.
*Bos.* A barren, beggarly virtue.
*Duch.* I prithee, who is greatest? can you tell?
Sad tales befit my woe: I'll tell you one.
A salmon, as she swam unto the sea,
Met with a dog-fish, who encounters her
With this rough language: 'Why art thou so bold
To mix thyself with our high state of floods,
Being no eminent courtier, but one
That for the calmest and fresh time o'th' year
Dost live in shallow rivers, rank'st thyself
With silly smelts and shrimps? and darest thou
Pass by our dog-ship, without reverence?'
'O', quoth the salmon, 'sister, be at peace:
Thank Jupiter we both have pass'd the net!

***118. counterfeit face:*** the mask that conceals his real face. Alternatively, though she does not recognise him at first (l.100: 'what devil art thou') she has now seen through the disguise and she contrasts the counterfeit or false sympathy of Bosola in the earlier scenes with his true real nature here. ***125–39. A salmon...fire:*** See note to III.ii.122–35. ***132. smelts:*** small fish.

Our value never can be truly known
Till in the fisher's basket we be shown;
I'th' market then my price may be the higher,
Even when I am nearest to the cook and fire.'
So, to great men, the moral may be stretched:
*Men oft are valued high, when th'are most wretched.*
But come; whither you please: I am arm'd'gainst misery;
Bent to all sways of the oppressor's will.
*There's no deep valley, but near some great hill.* *Exeunt.*

# ACT IV

## Scene i

*Enter* FERDINAND *and* BOSOLA.

*Ferd.* How doth our sister duchess bear herself
In her imprisonment?
*Bos.* Nobly; I'll describe her:
She's sad, as one long us'd to't; and she seems
Rather to welcome the end of misery
Than shun it:—a behaviour so noble
As gives a majesty to adversity;
You may discern the shape of loveliness
More perfect in her tears, than in her smiles;
She will muse four hours together, and her silence,
Methinks, expresseth more than if she spake.
*Ferd.* Her melancholy seems to be fortify'd
With a strange disdain.
*Bos.* 'Tis so: and this restraint
(Like English mastiffs, that grow fierce with tying)
Makes her too passionately apprehend
Those pleasures she's kept from.
*Ferd.* Curse upon her!
I will no longer study in the book
Of another's heart: inform her what I told you. *Exit.*

*Enter* Duchess.

*Bos.* All comfort to your grace!
*Duch.* I will have none:—
Pray thee, why dost thou wrap thy poison'd pills
In gold and sugar?
*Bos.* Your elder brother, the Lord Ferdinand,
Is come to visit you: and sends you word,
'Cause once he rashly made a solemn vow
Never to see you more, he comes i'th' night;
And prays you, gently, neither torch nor taper

**2. *imprisonment:*** confined within her palace.

Shine in your chamber: he will kiss your hand,
And reconcile himself; but, for his vow,
He dares not see you:—

*Duch.* At his pleasure;
Take hence the lights: [*Bosola removes lights.*]

[*Enter* FERDINAND.]

he's come.

*Ferd.* Where are you?

*Duch.* Here sir:—

*Ferd.* This darkness suits you well.

*Duch.* I would ask you pardon:—

*Ferd.* You have it;
For I account it the honourabl'st revenge,
Where I may kill, to pardon:—where are your cubs?

*Duch.* Whom?

*Ferd.* Call them your children;
For though our national law distinguish bastards
From true legitimate issue, compassionate nature
Makes them all equal.

*Duch.* Do you visit me for this?
You violate a sacrament o'th' church
Shall make you howl in hell for't.

*Ferd.* It had been well
Could you have liv'd thus always; for indeed
You were too much i'th' light:—but no more—
I come to seal my peace with you: here's a hand.
*Gives her a dead man's hand.*
To which you vow'd much love; the ring upon't
You gave.

*Duch.* I affectionately kiss it.

*Ferd.* Pray do: and bury the print of it in your heart:
I will leave this ring with you for a love-token;
And the hand, as sure as the ring; and do not doubt
But you shall have the heart too; when you need a friend
Send it to him that ow'd it; you shall see
Whether he can aid you.

***43. S.D. Gives her a dead man's hand.*** The mental tortures begin. ***49. you shall... too:*** double-entendre with terrible irony. ***50. ow'd it:*** owned.

*Duch.* You are very cold.
I fear you are not well after your travel:—
Hah! lights!—O, horrible!
*Ferd.* Let her have lights enough. *Exit.*
*Duch.* What witchcraft doth he practise that he hath left
A dead man's hand here?—
*Here is discovered, behind a traverse, the artificial figures of Antonio and his children, appearing as if they were dead.*
*Bos.* Look you: here's the piece from which 't was ta'en:
He doth present you this sad spectacle
That now you know directly they are dead—
Hereafter you may wisely cease to grieve
For that which cannot be recovered.
*Duch.* There is not between heaven and earth one wish
I stay for after this: it wastes me more
Than were't my picture, fashion'd out of wax,
Stuck with a magical needle and then buried
In some foul dunghill; and yon's an excellent property
For a tyrant, which I would account mercy.
*Bos.* What's that?
*Duch.* If they would bind me to that lifeless trunk,
And let me freeze to death.
*Bos.* Come, you must live.
*Duch.* That's the greatest torture souls feel in hell—
In hell: that they must live, and cannot die.
Portia, I'll new-kindle thy coals again,
And revive the rare and almost dead example
Of a loving wife.
*Bos.* O fie! despair? remember
You are a Christian.
*Duch.* The church enjoins fasting:
I'll starve myself to death.
*Bos.* Leave this vain sorrow:

*55. **traverse:*** curtain. *63–4. **my picture…magical needle:*** In medieval witchcraft, wax effigies of people were pierced with needles and it was believed that they would experience the pain and eventually waste away. *72. **Portia:*** wife of Brutus. There was a story narrated by Plutarch, that after the death of Brutus she put hot coals in her mouth to choke herself to death.

Things being at the worst begin to mend;
The bee when he hath shot his sting into your hand
May then play with your eyelid.

*Duch.* Good comfortable fellow
Persuade a wretch that's broke upon the wheel
To have all his bones new set; entreat him live
To be executed again:—who must despatch me?
I account this world a tedious theatre,
For I do play a part in't 'gainst my will.

*Bos.* Come, be of comfort, I will save your life.

*Duch.* Indeed I have not leisure to tend so small a business.

*Bos.* Now, by my life, I pity you.

*Duch.* Thou art a fool then,
To waste thy pity on a thing so wretch'd
As cannot pity itself:—I am full of daggers:
Puff: let me blow these vipers from me.

*Enter* Servant.

What are you?

*Serv.* One that wishes you long life.

*Duch.* I would thou wert hang'd for the horrible curse
Thou hast given me: [*Exit* Servant.]
I shall shortly grow one
Of the miracles of pity:—I'll go pray: no,
I'll go curse:—

*Bos.* O fie!

*Duch.* I could curse the stars.

*Bos.* O fearful!

*Duch.* And those three smiling seasons of the year

***81. wheel:*** a form of torture. ***85. For I do play...will:*** cf. *Merchant of Venice* (I.i.77–9): 'I hold the world but as the world. Gratiano. A stage where every man must play a part/ And mine a sad one. ***91–4. S.D. Enter Servant...Exit Servant:*** This passage seems pointless unless we presume that Ferdinand has sent him to see how the Duchess is faring. But there is no indication in the text that this is so. The remark 'One that wishes you a long life' just after she has declared that she lives against her will (l.85) is, however, full of cruel dramatic irony. Webster has perhaps sacrificed logical verisimilitude for symbolic stylisation, the anonymous servant representing a world where everyone is against her and nothing makes sense any more. ***96–100. I could curse the stars...shine still:*** The Duchess's curse against the stars is in the vein of similar agonised curses against the universe, delivered by Shakespeare's Lear (III.ii.4–9), and Timor (IV.iii.1–6) in their moments of crisis. Bosola's comment is a pitilessly ironic remark. The stars are unaffected by her curse, the heavens are unconcerned, unmoved at her plight and the

Into a Russian winter, nay the world
To its first chaos.

*Bos.* Look you, the stars shine still:—

*Duch.* O, but you must
Remember, my curse hath a great way to go.—
Plagues, that make lanes through largest families,
Consume them!—

*Bos.* Fie lady!

*Duch.* Let them, like tyrants,
Never be remember'd, but for the ill they have done;
Let all the zealous prayers of mortified
Churchmen forget them!—

*Bos.* O, uncharitable!

*Duch.* Let heaven, a little while, cease crowning martyrs,
To punish them!
Go howl them this: and say I long to bleed:
It is some mercy, when men kill with speed. *Exit.*

[*Enter* FERDINAND.]

*Ferd.* Excellent: as I would wish; she's plagu'd in art.
These presentations are but fram'd in wax,
By the curious master in that quality,
Vincentio Lauriola, and she takes them
For true substantial bodies.

*Bos.* Why do you do this?

remark suggests a mocking negation of compassion in the universe. Bosola is deliberately teasing, if not needling the Duchess in his cat-and-mouse game with her and the line acquired more dramatic force possibly when the original actor of Bosola (John Lowin) deifically gestured towards the 'heavens' of the Globe Theatre. Yet though intended to be in a ruthless hostile spirit, there could be a degree of ambivalence in the line as if Bosola half-fearfully, half-defiantly, is expecting the stars to strike him down any moment. One may recall the crazed lover of Porphyria in Browning's *Porphyria's Lover* who, having strangled her says, in almost the same half-fearful, half-defiant manner: 'And yet God has not said a word'. This is the only way we can accommodate Ellis-Fermor's comments on the line in *The Jacobean Drama* (Methuen 1936). She quotes it twice (ch.1, p.4: 'The resolution is complete in Shakespeare's latest plays ... "Look you, the stars shine still." They do indeed' and ch. 4, para 1). On the face of it, Ellis-Fermor seems to suggest that the remark is an assertion and affirmation of a divine providence that lies beyond the tragedy of life. If this is what she means then she has, incredible as it may seem, totally misinterpreted the meaning of the words. ***111. in art:*** The dead figures are wax effigies, created by art.

*Ferd.* To bring her to despair.
*Bos.* Faith, end here:
And go no farther in your cruelty—
Send her a penitential garment to put on
Next to her delicate skin, and furnish her
With beads and prayer-books.
*Ferd.* Damn her! that body of hers,
While that my blood ran pure in't, was more worth
Than that which thou wouldst comfort, call'd a soul—
I will send her masques of common courtesans,
Have her meat serv'd up by bawds and ruffians,
And, 'cause she'll needs be mad, I am resolv'd
To remove forth the common hospital
All the mad-folk, and place them near her lodging;
There let them practise together, sing, and dance,
And act their gambols to the full o'th' moon:
If she can sleep the better for it, let her—
Your work is almost ended.
*Bos.* Must I see her again?
*Ferd.* Yes.
*Bos.* Never.
*Ferd.* You must.
*Bos.* Never in mine own shape,
That's forfeited by my intelligence,
And this last cruel lie: when you send me next,
The business shall be comfort.
*Ferd.* Very likely—
Thy pity is nothing of kin to thee:—Antonio
Lurks about Milan; thou shalt shortly thither
To feed a fire, as great as my revenge,
Which ne'er will slack, till it have spent his fuel:
*Intemperate agues make physicians cruel.* *Exeunt.*

***116. to despair:*** despair that will lead to madness. See l. 126 below. ***117–21. Faith end…prayer books:*** Bosola's pity for the Duchess seems genuine here. See the analysis of his character in the Introduction to the Play. ***119. penitential garment:*** like a hair-shirt that bites and scratches into the skin. Note Ferdinand's violent reaction against anything that could mar her beauty. See the analysis of his character in the Introduction to the play. ***130. the full o' th' moon:*** The popular belief that the full moon affected people and drove them mad is evident in the fact that the word 'lunatic' is derived from the Latin 'lunaticus', from 'luna' (moon). ***136. cruel lie:*** deceiving her with the wax effigies.

## Scene ii

*Enter* Duchess *and* CARIOLA.

*Duch.* What hideous noise was that?
*Cari.* 'Tis the wild consort
Of madmen, lady, which your tyrant brother
Hath plac'd about your lodging:—this tyranny,
I think, was never practis'd till this hour.
*Duch.* Indeed I thank him: nothing but noise and folly
Can keep me in my right wits, whereas reason
And silence make me stark mad:— sit down;
Discourse to me some dismal tragedy.
*Cari.* O, 'twill increase your melancholy.
*Duch.* Thou art deceiv'd,
To hear of greater grief would lessen mine—
This is a prison?
*Cari.* Yes, but you shall live
To shake this durance off.
*Duch.* Thou art a fool;
The robin-redbreast, and the nightingale,
Never live long in cages.
*Cari.* Pray dry your eyes.
What think you of, madam?
*Duch.* Of nothing:
When I muse thus, I sleep.
*Cari.* Like a madman, with your eyes open?
*Duch.* Dost thou think we shall know one another,
In th'other world?
*Cari.* Yes, out of question.
*Duch.* O that it were possible we might
But hold some two days' conference with the dead,
From them I should learn somewhat, I am sure

*1. consort:* group. *14. pray dry your eyes:* As with Shakespeare, stage directions are often incorporated within the speeches of the characters. Cf. *Macbeth*, IV.iii.208): 'What, man! ne' er pull your hat upon your brows.' *18. we shall...one another:* referring specifically to Antonio, not a general observation.

I never shall know here:—I'll tell thee a miracle—
I am not mad yet, to my cause of sorrow.
Th' heaven o'er my head seems made of molten brass,
The earth of flaming sulphur, yet I am not mad:
I am acquainted with sad misery,
As the tann'd galley-slave is with his oar;
Necessity makes me suffer constantly,
And custom makes it easy—who do I look like now?

*Cari.* Like to your picture in the gallery,
A deal of life in show, but none in practice;
Or rather like some reverend monument
Whose ruins are even pitied.

*Duch.* Very proper:
And Fortune seems only to have her eyesight
To behold my tragedy:—How now!
What noise is that?

*Enter* Servant.

*Serv.* I am come to tell you
Your brother hath intended you some sport:
A great physician, when the Pope was sick
Of a deep melancholy, presented him
With several sorts of madmen, which wild object,
Being full of change and sport, forc'd him to laugh,
And so th' imposthume broke: the self-same cure
The duke intends on you.

*Duch.* Let them come in.

*Serv.* There's a mad lawyer, and a secular priest,
A doctor that hath forfeited his wits
By jealousy; an astrologian
That in his works said such a day o'th' month
Should be the day of doom, and failing of 't,
Ran mad; an English tailor, craz'd i'th brain
With the study of new fashion; a gentleman usher

***35–6. And Fortune… tragedy:*** a hint of fatalism or determinism that is unusual for the Duchess. ***43. imposthume:*** abscess. ***45. secular priest:*** a priest who moves about in the community and does not live in monastic seclusion. ***45–111. There's a mad lawyer… master-piece:*** The order in which the servant describes the madmen is not maintained in the speeches that follow. Nor is it always possible to identify the madmen from their

Quite beside himself, with care to keep in mind
The number of his lady's salutations,
Or 'How do you', she employ'd him in each morning;
A farmer too, an excellent knave in grain,
Mad 'cause he was hinder'd transportation:
And let one broker that's mad loose to these,
You'd think the devil were among them.

*Duch.* Sit Cariola: Let them loose when you please,
For I am chain'd to endure all your tyranny.

*Enter* Madmen.

*Here, by a* Madman, *this song is sung, to a dismal kind of music.*

*O, let us howl, some heavy note,*
*Some deadly dogged howl,*
*Sounding as from the threat'ning throat*
*Of beasts, and fatal fowl!*
*As ravens, screech-owls, bulls, and bears,*
*We'll bill and bawl our parts,*
*Till irksome noise have cloy'd your ears*
*And corrosiv'd your hearts.*
*At last when as our choir wants breath,*
*Our bodies being blest,*
*We'll sing like swans, to welcome death,*
*And die in love and rest.*

*Ist Madman.* Doomsday not come yet? I'll draw it nearer by a perspective, or make a glass that shall set all the

speeches. This confusion or disorder symbolically repeats the disorder in their minds and the disorder in the universe as a whole. There are eight madmen—lawyer, priest, doctor, astrologer, tailor, gentleman-usher, farmer, and broker. According to the text, only four madmen, designated $1^{st}$, $2^{nd}$, $3^{rd}$ and $4^{th}$, speak, but this may not mean that only the same four madmen speak. The textual notes that follow will make this clear. There is a sexual innuendo running through most of the speeches which seems to relate to that which is foremost in Ferdinand's mind, for Ferdinand is obsessed, to a psychopathic degree with sex. The recurring images of fire, hell and sleeplessness could also apply to Ferdinand who is consumed by the fire of his own passion: It is almost as if the madmen are variants of Ferdinand himself, who becomes totally mad in the last act. Compare the damned souls in the drunken porter's speech, in *Macbeth*, all of whom represent Macbeth. Among them also, there is a tailor and a farmer. ***73–6. Doomsday... porcupines:*** This is obviously the mad astrologer. ***74. perspective:*** telescope, which seems to make distant objects come near. ***74. glass*:** magnifying glass, which, if held against the sun, can start a fire.

world on fire upon an instant: I cannot sleep; my pillow is stuffed with a litter of porcupines.

*2nd Madman.* Hell is a mere glass-house, where the devils are continually blowing up women's souls, on hollow irons, and the fire never goes out.

*3rd Madman.* I will lie with every woman in my parish the tenth night: I will tythe them over, like hay-cocks.

*4th Madman.* Shall my pothecary outgo me, because I am a cuckold? I have found out his roguery: he makes alum of his wife's urine, and sells it to puritans that have sore throats with over-straining.

*1st Madman.* I have skill in heraldry.

*2nd Madman.* Hast?

*1st Madman.* You do give for your crest a woodcock's head, with the brains picked out on't—you are a very ancient gentleman.

*3rd Madman.* Greek is turned Turk; we are only to be saved by the Helvetian translation.

***77–9. Hell... goes out:*** There is a mad logic in the way a madman often picks up a word or an idea from the previous speech and then goes off at a tangent with his own thoughts. 'Glass' (l.74) leads the 2nd madman on to 'glass-house'. ***77. glass-house:*** glass-blowing factory. Cf. II.ii.9–11, where blown glass is likened to a pregnant woman's belly. The word 'women' (l.78) leads on to the speech of the 3rd madman who is obviously the 'secular priest'. ***81. tythe:*** originally the tenth part of one's produce which had to be given to the church. The priest will have his 'tythe' or share of the women in the parish. ***81. hay-cocks:*** hay-stacks. ***82–5. 4th Madman...overstraining:*** The 4th madman is consistently the doctor. The husbands of the women the priest sleeps with are cuckolds. ***83. alum:*** medicine. ***84. puritans:*** the secular priest is probably a Puritan. ***86. heraldry:*** science dealing with coats of arms and crests of noble families. This leads on to the 'crest' of l.88, where it also means the tuft of feathers on a woodcock's head. ***88. woodcock:*** a term often used for fools, without brains. ***91–2. Greek...translation:*** The 3rd madman is still the priest. The word 'ancient' used in the previous line may have led the priest on to think of the 'ancient' or earliest Greek translation of the Old Testament in the 3rd century BC (from the original Hebrew) and the New Testament in the 4th and 5th centuries AD. The New Testament was first translated into English from the Greek text by William Tyndale. From 1537 a number of translations were made by Protestant reformers. In the reign of Queen Mary, an ardent Catholic, these reformers took refuge in Geneva where, in 1560, appeared the Genevan or 'Breeches' Bible'. It had a marginal commentary which appealed to the Puritans. This is the Helvetian translation that the priest refers to. The Authorised Version which appeared in 1611 was practically the Version of Tyndale. For the mad priest any translation that is closer to the Catholic faith is almost a heretical version and therefore 'turned Turk'.

*1st Madman.* Come on sir, I will lay the law to you.
*2nd Madman.* O, rather lay a corrosive; the law will eat to the bone.
*3rd Madman.* He that drinks but to satisfy nature is damned.
*4th Madman.* If I had my glass here, I would show a sight
should make all the women here call me mad doctor.
*1st Madman.* What's he, a rope-maker? [*Points at 3rd Madman.*]
*2nd Madman.* No, no, no, a snuffling knave, that while he
shows the tombs, will have his hand in a wench's
placket.
*3rd Madman.* Woe to the caroche, that brought home my wife
from the masque, at three o'clock in the morning!
it had a large featherbed in it.
*4th Madman.* I have pared the devil's nails forty times,
roasted them in raven's eggs, and cured agues with them.
*3rd Madman.* Get me three hundred milch-bats to make
possets, to procure sleep.
*4th Madman.* All the college may throw their caps at me, I
have made a soap-boiler costive—
it was my master-piece:—

*Here the dance, consisting of 8 Madmen, with music answerable thereunto; after which BOSOLA, like an old man, enters [and the Madmen leave].*

*Duch.* Is he mad too?
*Serv.* Pray question him: I'll leave you. [*Exit.*]
*Bos.* I am come to make thy tomb.
*Duch.* Hah, my tomb!
Thou speak'st as if I lay upon my death-bed,
Gasping for breath: dost thou perceive me sick?

***93. 1st Madman:*** He seems to be the lawyer rather than the astrologer here. ***93. lay:*** explain. ***95. 3rd Madman:*** He is still the priest. ***96. glass:*** beaker or medicinal vessel. ***98. 1st Madman:*** His identity here is not clearly indicated. The word 'damned' (95) spoken by the 3rd madman (the priest) leads to a 'rope-maker' or a hangman. ***99–101. while he... placket:*** Presumably the 3rd madman who 'shows the tombs' is still the lecherous priest. ***101. placket:*** petticoat or an opening on its side. ***102–3. Woe... morning:*** This speech cannot be attributed to the priest. ***102. caroche***: carriage. Sometimes they were fitted with beds. ***107–8. Get...sleep:*** again, unlikely to be the priest's words. ***107. milch bats:*** suckling bats. ***108. possets:*** medicinal drinks made with hot milk. ***109. college:*** of physicians. ***109. throw their caps:*** run after me, from either emulation or envy. ***110. soap-boiler:*** soap-maker. ***110. costive:*** constipated.

*Bos.* Yes, and the more dangerously, since thy sickness is insensible.

*Duch.* Thou art not mad, sure—dost know me?

*Bos.* Yes.

*Duch.* Who am I?

*Bos.* Thou art a box of worm-seed, at best, but a salvatory of green mummy:—what's this flesh? a little crudded milk, fantastical puff-paste; our bodies are weaker than those paper prisons boys use to keep flies in; more contemptible, since ours is to preserve earth-worms. Didst thou ever see a lark in a cage? such is the soul in the body: this world is like her little turf of grass, and the heaven o'er our heads, like her looking-glass, only gives us a miserable knowledge of the small compass of our prison.

*Duch.* Am not I thy duchess?

*Bos.* Thou art some great woman, sure, for riot begins to sit on thy forehead, clad in gray hairs, twenty years sooner than on a merry milkmaid's. Thou sleepest worse than if a mouse should be forced to take up her lodging in a cat's ear: a little infant that breeds its teeth, should it lie with thee, would cry out, as if thou wert the more unquiet bedfellow.

*Duch.* I am Duchess of Malfi still.

*Bos.* That makes thy sleeps so broken:
*Glories, like glow-worms, afar off shine bright,*
*But look'd to near, have neither heat, nor light.*

*Duch.* Thou art very plain.

*Bos.* My trade is to flatter the dead, not the living—

***121. worm-seed:*** dried seeds used medicinally to cure worms in the intestines. ***121. salvatory:*** a container for ointments. ***122. green mummy:*** medicinal ointment made from preserved dead bodies or mummies. ***122. green:*** the colour is evocative of the lividness of putrefying flesh. ***122. crudded:*** curdled. ***123. fantastical:*** grotesque. ***125. earth-worms:*** Cf. Marvell, 'To his Coy Mistress': ' then worms shall try / That long preserv'd Virginity'. ***126–30. Didst... our prison:*** Bosola universalises the Duchess's imprisoned condition to draw a philosophic conclusion on human existence. ***132. riot:*** confusion or lines of sadness and care. ***135–6. a mouse...ear:*** with fear and trepidation. ***138. the more unquiet bed fellow:*** ironically echoes Cariola's 'the sprawling'st bed-fellow (III.ii.13). ***141–2. Glories...light:*** These lines are repeated from *W.D.* V. i.41–2.

I am a tomb-maker.
*Duch.* And thou comest to make my tomb?
*Bos.* Yes.
*Duch.* Let me be a little merry—of what stuff wilt thou make it?
*Bos.* Nay, resolve me first, of what fashion?
*Duch.* Why, do we grow fantastical in our death-bed?
do we affect fashion in the grave?
*Bos.* Most ambitiously: princes' images on their tombs do
not lie, as they were wont, seeming to pray up to
heaven, but with their hands under their cheeks,
as if they died of the tooth-ache; they are not
carved with their eyes fixed upon the stars,
but as their minds were wholly bent upon the world,
the selfsame way they seem to turn their faces.
*Duch.* Let me know fully therefore the effect
Of this thy dismal preparation,
This talk fit for a charnel.
*Bos.* Now I shall:

*Enter* Executioners *[with] a coffin, cords and a bell.*

Here is a present from your princely brothers,
And may it arrive welcome, for it brings
Last benefit, last sorrow.
*Duch.* Let me see it—
I have so much obedience in my blood,
I wish it in their veins, to do them good.
*Bos.* This is your last presence-chamber.
*Cari.* O my sweet lady!
*Duch.* Peace, it affrights not me.
*Bos.* I am the common bellman

***152–8. princes' images… faces:*** Fashions in tomb-making, that had started by the end of the 16th century in England are indicative of the new materialism that made people concern themselves only with this life. In Renaissance Italy this kind of worldly activity was the height of fashion. Compare Browning's *The Bishop Orders His Tomb at St. Praxed's*. ***161. charnel:*** charnel-house where dead bodies are kept. ***167. presence-chamber:*** audience-hall. ***169. bellman:*** In 1605, Master Robert Dove or Dowe presented a charity to the church of St. Sepulchre near Newgate prison whereby a bellman was paid to ring a bell outside the cell when condemned prisoners were to be hanged the next morning. This was to remind them of their imminent death so that they might pray to the Lord to save their souls; cf. *Macbeth* (II.ii.3–4): 'It was the owl that shriek'd, the fatal bellman/ Which gives the stern'st good-night.'

That usually is sent to condemn'd persons
The night before they suffer:—

*Duch.* Even now thou said'st
Thou wast a tomb-maker.

*Bos.* 'Twas to bring you
By degrees to mortification. Listen:
*Hark, now everything is still,*
*The screech-owl, and the whistler shrill*
*Call upon our dame, aloud,*
*And bid her quickly don her shroud.*
*Much you had of land and rent,*
*Your length in clay's now competent.*
*A long war disturb'd your mind*
*Here your perfect peace is sign'd.*
*Of what is't fools make such vain keeping?*
*Sin their conception, their birth weeping;*
*Their life a general mist of error,*
*Their death a hideous storm of terror.*
*Strew your hair with powders sweet,*
*Don clean linen, bathe your feet,*
*And (the foul fiend more to check)*
*A crucifix let bless your neck.*
*'Tis now full tide,'tween night and day:*
*End your groan, and come away.*

*Cari.* Hence villains, tyrants, murderers! Alas!
What will you do with my lady? call for help.

*Duch.* To whom? To our next neighbours? they are mad-folks.

*Bos.* Remove that noise.

*Duch.* Farewell Cariola:
In my last will I have not much to give;
A many hungry guests have fed upon me,
Thine will be a poor reversion.

*Cari.* I will die with her.

*Duch.* I pray thee, look thou giv'st my little boy

***173. mortification:*** reducing the mind to a state of mental inaction preparatory for death. ***177. shroud:*** winding sheet for dead bodies. ***179. competent:*** enough. ***184. mist:*** a favourite word of Webster, used in both *W. D* and *D.M.* ***198. reversion:*** inheritance, legacy. ***199–201. I pray thee... she sleep:*** This remark, suggesting the trivial domesticity of a mother giving instructions to the maid while she goes out for the day, could seem somewhat sweetly saccharine in the context of the stark tragedy of the

Some syrup for his cold, and let the girl
Say her prayers, ere she sleep.
[*Executioners force* CARIOLA *off.*]
Now what you please—
What death?

*Bos.* Strangling: here are your executioners.

*Duch.* I forgive them:
The apoplexy, catarrh, or cough o'th' lungs
Would do as much as they do.

*Bos.* Doth not death fright you?

*Duch.* Who would be afraid on't?
Knowing to meet such excellent company
In th' other world.

*Bos.* Yet, methinks,
The manner of your death should much afflict you,
This cord should terrify you?

*Duch.* Not a whit:
What would it pleasure me to have my throat cut
With diamonds? Or to be smothered
With cassia? Or to be shot to death with pearls?
I know death hath ten thousand several doors
For men to take their exits; and 'tis found
They go on such strange geometrical hinges,
You may open them both ways: —any way, for heaven-sake,
So I were out of your whispering: —tell my brothers
That I perceive death, now I am well awake,
Best gift is they can give, or I can take.
I would fain put off my last woman's fault,
I'd not be tedious to you.

*Execut.* We are ready.

*Duch.* Dispose my breath how please you, but my body

moment. But at the same time it is psychologically not implausible that at the hour of death the Duchess cannot cope with its enormity and clings—for sanity—to the trivial little details of homely day-to-day life. It also brings out the essential femininity in her. ***204. apoplexy:*** stroke. ***204. catarrh:*** formerly a term used to refer to cerebral haemorrhage. ***217. geometrical hinges:*** hinges suggest doors that can swing either way, but the meaning is not clear. It could mean that someone can pull it for her or she can push it open herself (i.e. suicide).

Bestow upon my women, will you?

*Execut.* Yes.

*Duch.* Pull, and pull strongly, for your able strength
Must pull down heaven upon me:—
Yet stay; heaven-gates are not so highly arch'd
As princes' palaces, they that enter there
Must go upon their knees.—[*Kneels.*] Come violent death,
Serve for mandragora to make me sleep!
Go tell my brothers, when I am laid out,
They then may feed in quiet. *They strangle her.*

*Bos.* Where's the waiting woman?
Fetch her: some other strangle the children.

[Executioners *fetch* CARIOLA, *and one goes to strangle the children.*]

Look you, there sleeps your mistress.

*Cari.* O, you are damn'd
Perpetually for this:—my turn is next,
Is't not so order'd?

*Bos.* Yes, and I am glad
You are so well prepar'd for't.

*Cari.* You are deceiv'd sir,
I am not prepar'd for't, I will not die;
I will first come to my answer, and know
How I have offended.

*Bos.* Come, despatch her:—
You kept her counsel, now you shall keep ours.

*Cari.* I will not die, I must not, I am contracted
To a young gentleman.

*Execut.* Here's your wedding r

*Cari.* Let me but speak with the duke: I'll disco
Treason to his person.

*Bos.* Delays:—thro

*Execut.* She bites, and scratches:—

**231. *mandragora:*** mandrake. Shakespeare first uses ... *Othello* (III.iii.335–6): 'not poppy, nor mandragora ... world'. ***233. They then ... quiet:*** ironical. They wi... ***241. I will first...answer.*** legally defend myself ... noose of the rope.

narcotic in ... syrups of the ... eace of mind. ... *dding ring:* the

*Cari.* If you kill me now
I am damn'd: I have not been at confession
This two years:—

*Bos.* When?

*Cari.* I am quick with child.

*Bos.* Why then,
Your credit's sav'd:—[*The* Executioners *strangle Cariola.*]
bear her into th' next room;
Let this lie still.

[*Exeunt* Executioners *with the body of Cariola.*]

*Enter* FERDINAND.

*Ferd.* Is she dead?

*Bos.* She is what
You'd have her: but here begin your pity—
*Shows the children strangled.*
Alas, how have these offended?

*Ferd.* The death
Of young wolves is never to be pitied.

*Bos.* Fix your eye here:—

*Ferd.* Constantly.

*Bos.* Do you not weep?
Other sins only speak; murder shrieks out:
The element of water moistens the earth,
But blood flies upwards, and bedews the heavens.

*Ferd.* Cover her face: mine eyes dazzle: she died young.

*Bos.* I think not so: her infelicity
Seem'd to have years too many.

*Fer[d].* She and I were twins:
And should I die this instant, I had liv'd
Her time to a minute.

260. pers[…]*face... young:* Although no critic has commented on this, when a tong[…] the face becomes bloated and mottled, the eyes stare out and the factu[…]or artistic reasons perhaps Webster deliberately disregarded this disto[…]is no indication either way in the text. In any case, the physical Subse[…] would not be great, because she is not quite dead yet. 'Merc[…]pes' (l.343) and 86 lines after she has been strangled she cries beaut[…]e powerful drama that Ferdinand cannot bear to see the […]d. ***261–2. her infelicity…many:*** she is old in suffering.

That I may never see thee.

*Bos.* Let me know
Wherefore I should be thus neglected? sir,
I serv'd your tyranny; and rather strove
To satisfy yourself, than all the world;
And though I loath'd the evil, yet I lov'd
You that did counsel it; and rather sought
To appear a true servant, than an honest man.

*Ferd.* I'll go hunt the badger, by owl-light:
'Tis a deed of darkness. *Exit.*

*Bos.* He's much distracted:—off my painted honour:
While with vain hopes our faculties we tire,
We seem to sweat in ice, and freeze in fire.
What would I do, were this to do again?
I would not change my peace of conscience
For all the wealth of Europe:—she stirs; here's life:
Return, fair soul, from darkness, and lead mine
Out of this sensible hell:—she's warm, she breathes:—
Upon thy pale lips I will melt my heart
To store them with fresh colour:—who's there?
Some cordial drink!—Alas! I dare not call:
So pity would destroy pity:— her eye opes,
And heaven in it seems to ope, that late was shut,
To taken me up to mercy.

*Duch.* Antonio!

*Bos.* Yes, madam, he is living—
The dead bodies you saw were but feign'd statues;
He's reconcil'd to your brothers; the Pope hath wrought
The atonement.

*Duch.* Mercy! *She dies.*

*Bos.* O, she's gone again: there the cords of life broke.
O sacred innocence, that sweetly sleeps
On turtles' feathers, whilst a guilty conscience

***327–9. And though… honest man:*** Bosola's explanation also rings hollow. See Introduction, pp.xxxix–xli and also Bosola's own words: 'off my painted honour' (l.332). ***330–1. I'll go hunt…darkness:*** perhaps the beginning of the madness that overtakes him in Act.V. ***332. painted:*** affected, false. ***343. pity… pity:*** His call for pity might bring back Ferdinand and thus destroy the pity. ***349. atonement:*** reconciliation. ***352. turtle:*** turtle-dove. Cf. *Song of Solomon*, ch. 2, 12: 'The voice of the turtle is heard in our land.'

Is a black register, wherein is writ
All our good deeds and bad, a perspective
That shows us hell! That we cannot be suffer'd
To do good when we have a mind to it!
This is manly sorrow:
These tears, I am very certain, never grew
In my mother's milk. My estate is sunk
Below the degree of fear: where were
These penitent fountains while she was living?
O, they were frozen up! Here is a sight
As direful to my soul as is the sword
Unto a wretch hath slain his father. Come,
I'll bear thee hence:
And execute thy last will; that's deliver
Thy body to the reverent dispose
Of some good women: that the cruel tyrant
Shall not deny me. Then I'll post to Milan
Where somewhat I will speedily enact
Worth my dejection. *Exit* [, *with the body of the* Duchess].

***358–61. These tears...living:*** These words of repentance are sincere enough. Bosola is always sincere in any role he adopts, but how long the mood will last is another matter. He is ready to do more evil deeds in Act V. ***371. Worth my dejection:*** either 'in keeping with my sorrow' or 'do something about this humiliation I have faced'.

# ACT V

## Scene i

*Enter* ANTONIO *and* DELIO.

*Ant.* What think you of my hope of reconcilement
To the Arragonian brethren?

*Delio.* I misdoubt it,
For though they have sent their letters of safe conduct
For your repair to Milan, they appear
But nets to entrap you: the Marquis of Pescara,
Under whom you hold certain land in cheat,
Much 'gainst his noble nature, hath been mov'd
To seize those lands, and some of his dependants
Are at this instant making it their suit
To be invested in your revenues.
I cannot think they mean well to your life
That do deprive you of your means of life,
Your living.

*Ant.* You are still an heretic
To any safety I can shape myself.

*Enter* PESCARA.

*Delio.* Here comes the Marquis: I will make myself
Petitioner for some part of your land,
To know whither it is flying.

*Ant.* I pray do. [*He retires.*]

*Delio.* Sir, I have a suit to you.

*Pes.* To me ?

*Delio.* An easy one:
There is the Citadel of Saint Bennet,
With some demesnes, of late in the possession
Of Antonio Bologna—please you bestow them on me?

*Pes.* You are my friend: but this is such a suit,

***6. in cheat:*** in escheat (a legal term), meaning under certain conditions. ***10. be invested:*** receive. ***13. heretic:*** sceptical, therefore opposed to accepted belief.

Nor fit for me to give, nor you to take.

*Delio.* No sir?

*Pes.* I will give you ample reason for't
Soon in private:—

*Enter* JULIA.

here's the cardinal's mistress.

*Julia.* My lord, I am grown your poor petitioner,
And should be an ill beggar, had I not
A great man's letter here, the cardinal's
To court you in my favour. [*Gives letter.*]

*Pes.* He entreats for you
The Citadel of Saint Bennet, that belong'd
To the banish'd Bologna.

*Julia.* Yes.

*Pes.* I could not have thought of a friend I could
Rather pleasure with it: 'tis yours.

*Julia.* Sir, I thank you:
And he shall know how doubly I am engag'd
Both in your gift, and speediness of giving,
Which makes your grant the greater. *Exit.*

*Ant.* [*Aside*] How they fortify
Themselves with my ruin!

*Delio,* Sir, I am
Little bound to you.

*Pes.* Why?

*Delio.* Because you deny'd this suit to me, and gave't
To such a creature.

*Pes.* Do you know what it was?
It was Antonio's land: not forfeited
By course of law, but ravish'd from his throat
By the cardinal's entreaty: it were not fit
I should bestow so main a piece of wrong
Upon my friend; 'tis a gratification
Only due to a strumpet, for it is injustice.
Shall I sprinkle the pure blood of innocents
To make those followers I call my friends

Look ruddier upon me? I am glad
This land, ta'en from the owner by such wrong,
Returns again unto so foul an use
As salary for his lust. Learn, good Delio,
To ask noble things of me, and you shall find
I'll be a noble giver.

*Delio.* You instruct me well.

*Ant.* [*Aside*] Why, here's a man now, would fright impudence
From sauciest beggars.

*Pes.* Prince Ferdinand's come to Milan
Sick, as they give out, of an apoplexy;
But some say 'tis a frenzy: I am going
To visit him. *Exit.*

*Ant.* 'Tis a noble old fellow. [*He advances.*]

*Delio.* What course do you mean to take, Antonio?

*Ant.* This night I mean to venture all my fortune
(Which is no more than a poor ling'ring life)
To the cardinal's worst of malice: I have got
Private access to his chamber, and intend
To visit him, about the mid of night,
As once his brother did our noble duchess.
It may be that the sudden apprehension
Of danger—for I'll go in mine own shape—
When he shall see it fraught with love and duty,
May draw the poison out of him, and work
A friendly reconcilement: if it fail,
Yet it shall rid me of this infamous calling;
For better fall once, than be ever falling.

*Delio.* I'll second you in all danger: and how e'er,
My life keeps rank with yours.

*Ant.* You are still my lov'd, and best friend. *Exeunt.*

*49.* ***ruddier:*** more flushed with pleasure. *59.* ***frenzy:*** mental disorder. *73.* ***calling:*** my present condition. *75.* ***howe'er:*** whatever happens.

## Scene ii

*Enter* PESCARA *and a* Doctor.

*Pes.* Now doctor, may I visit your patient?
*Doc.* If't please your lordship: but he's instantly.
To take the air here in the gallery,
By my direction.
*Pes.* Pray thee, what's his disease?
*Doc.* A very pestilent disease, my lord,
They call lycanthropia.
*Pes.* What's that?
I need a dictionary to't.
*Doc.* I'll tell you:
In those that are possess'd with't there o'erflows
Such melancholy humour, they imagine
Themselves to be transformed into wolves,
Steal forth to churchyards in the dead of night,
And dig dead bodies up: as two nights since
One met the duke, 'bout midnight in a lane
Behind Saint Mark's church, with the leg of a man
Upon his shoulder; and he howl'd fearfully;
Said he was a wolf, only the difference
Was, a wolf's skin was hairy on the outside,
His on the inside; bade them take their swords,
Rip up his flesh, and try: straight I was sent for,
And having minister'd to him, found his grace
Very well recovered.
*Pes.* I am glad on't.
*Doc.* Yet not without some fear
Of a relapse. If he grow to his fit again
I'll go a nearer way to work with him
Than ever Paracelsus dream'd of: if

*6.* ***lycanthropia:*** the word, derived from Greek, was first used in English in 1594. A kind of insanity in which the victim imagines himself to be a wolf. *24.* ***nearer:*** more direct. *25.* ***Paracelsus:*** a famous Swiss physician (1493–1541) who wandered from country to country practising alchemy, magic and astrology. He is supposed to have initiated modern chemistry. Browning wrote a dramatic poem on him.

They'll give me leave I'll buffet his madness out of him.

*Enter* FERDINAND, MALATESTE, *and* Cardinal; BOSOLA [*follows and watches, apart*].

Stand aside: he comes.

*Ferd.* Leave me.

*Mal.* Why doth your lordship love this solitariness?

*Ferd.* Eagles commonly fly alone: they are crows, daws, and starlings that flock together:—look, what's that follows me?

*Mal.* Nothing, my lord.

*Ferd.* Yes:—

*Mal.* 'Tis your shadow.

*Ferd.* Stay it, let it not haunt me.

*Mal.* Impossible: if you move, and the sun shine:—

*Ferd.* I will throttle it. [*Throws himself down on his shadow.*]

*Mal.* O, my lord: you are angry with nothing.

*Ferd.* You are a fool: how is't possible I should catch my shadow unless I fall upon't? When I go to hell, I mean to carry a bribe; for look you, good gifts evermore make way for the worst persons.

*Pes.* Rise, good my lord.

*Ferd.* I am studying the art of patience.

*Pes.* 'Tis a noble virtue:—

*Ferd.* To drive six snails before me, from this town to Moscow; neither use goad nor whip to them, but let them take their own time:—the patientest man i'th' world match me for an experiment—and I'll crawl after like a sheep-biter.

*Card.* Force him up. [*They raise him.*]

*Ferd.* Use me well, you were best: what I have done, I have done: I'll confess nothing.

*Doc.* Now let me come to him:— are you mad, my lord? are you out of your princely wits?

*Ferd.* What's he?

***26. buffet:*** Whipping was supposed to be a cure for madness. ***51. sheep-biter:*** a dog that barks around sheep and worries them. ***53–4. what...nothing:*** It is this remark, probably, that makes the Cardinal afraid that Ferdinand, in his madness, will disclose all.

*Pes.* Your doctor.

*Ferd.* Let me have his beard sawed off, and his eyebrows filed more civil.

*Doc.* I must do mad tricks with him, for that's the only way on't. I have brought your grace a salamander's skin, to keep you from sun-burning.

*Ferd.* I have cruel sore eyes.

*Doc.* The white of a cockatrix's egg is present remedy.

*Ferd.* Let it be a new-laid one, you were best:—
Hide me from him; physicians are like kings,
They brook no contradiction.

*Doc.* Now he begins to fear me, now let me alone with him.

*Card.* How now, put off your gown!

*Doc.* Let me have some forty urinals filled with rose-water: he and I'll go pelt one another with them—now he begins to fear me:—can you fetch a frisk, sir?—Let him go, let him go upon my peril: I find by his eye, he stands in awe of me; I'll make him as tame as a dormouse.

*Ferd.* Can you fetch your frisks, sir?—I will stamp him into a cullis, flay off his skin, to cover one of the anatomies this rogue hath set i'th cold yonder, in Barber-Chirurgeons' Hall. Hence, hence, you are all of you like beasts for sacrifice; there's nothing left of you, but tongue, and belly, flattery, and lechery. [*Exit.*]

*Pes.* Doctor, he did not fear you throughly.

*Doc.* True, I was somewhat too forward. [*Exit.*]

*Bos.* Mercy upon me, what a fatal judgement
Hath fall'n upon this Ferdinand!

*Pes.* Knows your grace
What accident hath brought unto the prince
This strange distraction?

*Card.* [*Aside*] I must feign somewhat:—[*To them*] Thus they say it grew:

***62. salamander:*** See note to III.iii.49. ***65. cockatrix:*** See note to III.ii.87. ***77. fetch a frisk:*** a lively dance. ***78. cullis:*** broth, thick soup. ***78. anatomies:*** skeletons. ***79–80. Barber...Hall:*** a building in London, where dead bodies were preserved and displayed for medical students to dissect and analyse. ***82. S.D. Exit:*** The hasty departure of the discomfited doctor adds a touch of macabre humour to this scene.

You have heard it rumour'd for these many years,
None of our family dies, but there is seen
The shape of an old woman, which is given
By tradition to us to have been murder'd
By her nephews, for her riches; such a figure
One night, as the prince sat up late at's book,
Appear'd to him; when crying out for help,
The gentlemen of 's chamber found his grace
All on a cold sweat, alter'd much in face
And language; since which apparition,
He hath grown worse and worse, and I much fear
He cannot live.

*Bos.* Sir, I would speak with you.

*Pes.* We'll leave your grace,
Wishing to the sick prince, our noble lord,
All health of mind and body.

*Card.* You are most welcome.

[*Exeunt all except* Cardinal *and* BOSOLA.]

[*Aside*] Are you come? So:— this fellow must not know
By any means I had intelligence
In our duchess' death; for, though I counsell'd it,
The full of all th' engagement seem'd to grow
From Ferdinand. [*To him*] Now sir, how fares our sister?
I do not think but sorrow makes her look
Like to an oft-dy'd garment: she shall now
Taste comfort from me—why do you look so wildly?
O, the fortune of your master here, the prince,
Dejects you—but be you of happy comfort:
If you'll do one thing for me I'll entreat,
Though he had a cold tomb-stone o'er his bones,
I'd make you what you would be.

*Bos.* Any thing—
Give it me in a breath, and let me fly to't:
They that think long, small expedition win,
For musing much o'th' end, cannot begin.

*92. shape:* spectre, ghost. *108. engagement:* Bosola's appointment by, apparently, Ferdinand. *111. oft-dy'd garment:* shabby and old garment, repeatedly dyed. *116. a cold...bones:* even if he dies. *120. musing...begin:* too much thinking delays action.

*Enter* JULIA.

*Julia.* Sir, will you come in to supper?
*Card.* I am busy, leave me.
*Julia.* [*Aside*] What an excellent shape hath that fellow! *Exit.*
*Card.* 'Tis thus: Antonio lurks here in Milan;
Inquire him out, and kill him:—while he lives
Our sister cannot marry, and I have thought
Of an excellent match for her:—do this, and style me
Thy advancement.
*Bos.* But by what means shall I find him out?
*Card.* There is a gentleman, call'd Delio,
Here in the camp, that hath been long approv'd
His loyal friend: set eye upon that fellow,
Follow him to mass—may be Antonio,
Although he do account religion
But a school-name, for fashion of the world
May accompany him; or else go inquire out
Delio's confessor, and see if you can bribe
Him to reveal it; there are a thousand ways
A man might find to trace him; as to know
What fellows haunt the Jews for taking up
Great sums of money, for sure he's in want;
Or else to go to th' picture-makers and learn
Who bought her picture lately—some of these
Happily may take—
*Bos.* Well, I'll not freeze i'th' business;
I would see that wretched thing, Antonio,
Above all sights i'th world.
*Card.* Do, and be happy. *Exit.*
*Bos.* This fellow doth breed basilisks in's eyes,
He's nothing else but murder: yet he seems
Not to have notice of the duchess' death—
'Tis his cunning: I must follow his example;

***126–7. style...advancement:*** tell me what you want. ***134. school-name:*** Medieval theologians known as school men (from scholastic philosophy) lost their way in useless theorising over abstract knowledge. Erasmus ridiculed them in *In Praise of Folly* and Bacon criticised them for the futility of their logic in *Advancement of Learning,* i.e. Antonio is not a particularly religious person. ***139. Jews:*** known for money-lending.

There cannot be a surer way to trace
Than that of an old fox.

[*Enter* JULIA *pointing a pistol at him.*]

*Julia.* So, sir, you are well met.
*Bos.* How now?
*Julia.* Nay, the doors are fast enough:—
Now sir, I will make you confess your treachery.
*Bos.* Treachery?
*Julia.* Yes, confess to me
Which of my women 'twas you hir'd, to put
Love-powder into my drink?
*Bos.* Love-powder!
*Julia.* Yes,
When I was at Malfi—
Why should I fall in love with such a face else?
I have already suffer'd for thee so much pain,
The only remedy to do me good
Is to kill my longing.
*Bos.* Sure your pistol holds
Nothing but perfumes, or kissing-comfits.
Excellent lady,
You have a pretty way on't to discover
Your longing: come, come, I'll disarm you,
And arm you thus—yet this is wondrous strange.
*Julia.* Compare thy form, and my eyes together,
You'll find my love no such great miracle.
Now you'll say
I am wanton: this nice modesty in ladies
Is but a troublesome familiar
That haunts them.
*Bos.* Know you me, I am a blunt soldier.
*Julia.* The better—
Sure, there wants fire where there are no lively sparks

***150. trace:*** track, follow. ***151–223. So, sir...of silk:*** The entire scene is a grotesque parody of the wooing scene between the Duchess and Antonio. ***162. kissing-comfits:*** breath-sweeteners. ***166. arm:*** put my arm around you. ***170. nice:*** fastidious. ***171. troublesome familiars:*** a familiar spirit that accompanies witches. Compare the witches' familiars in *Macbeth,* I.i.

Of roughness.
*Bos.* And I want compliment.
*Julia.* Why ignorance
In courtship cannot make you do amiss,
If you have a heart to do well.
*Bos.* You are very fair.
*Julia.* Nay, if you lay beauty to my charge,
I must plead unguilty.
*Bos.* Your bright eyes
Carry a quiver of darts in them, sharper
Than sunbeams.
*Julia.* You will mar me with commendation,
Put yourself to the charge of courting me
Whereas now I woo you.
*Bos.* [*Aside*] I have it, I will work upon this creature—
[*To her*] Let us grow most amorously familiar:
If the great cardinal now should see me thus,
Would he not count me a villain?
*Julia.* No: he might count me a wanton,
Not lay a scruple of offence on you;
For if I see and steal a diamond,
The fault is not i'th' stone, but in me the thief
That purloins it:— I am sudden with you;
We that are great women of pleasure use to cut off
These uncertain wishes, and unquiet longings,
And in an instant join the sweet delight
And the pretty excuse together; had you been i'th' street,
Under my chamber window, even there
I should have courted you.
*Bos.* O, you are an excellent lady.
*Julia.* Bid me do somewhat for you presently,
To express I love you.
*Bos.* I will, and if you love me,
Fail not to effect it.
The cardinal is grown wondrous melancholy;
Demand the cause; let him not put you off

*175. **I want compliment:*** I lack courtly graces. *189. **scruple:*** minute amount. Scruple is a minute unit of apothecaries' weight equalling 20 grains or 1/24 ounce. *199. **presently:*** at once.

With feign'd excuse, discover the main ground on't.
*Julia.* Why would you know this?
*Bos.* I have depended on him,
And I hear that he is fall'n in some disgrace
With the Emperor—if he be, like the mice
That forsake falling houses, I would shift
To other dependance.
*Julia.* You shall not need follow the wars;
I'll be your maintenance.
*Bos.* And I your loyal servant—
But I cannot leave my calling.
*Julia.* Not leave
An ungrateful general, for the love of a sweet lady?
You are like some, cannot sleep in feather-beds,
But must have blocks for their pillows.
*Bos.* Will you do this?
*Julia.* Cunningly.
*Bos.* Tomorrow I'll expect th' intelligence.
*Julia.* Tomorrow? get you into my cabinet,
You shall have it with you: do not delay me,
No more than I do you; I am like one
That is condemn'd—I have my pardon promis'd,
But I would see it seal'd:—go, get you in,
You shall see me wind my tongue about his heart,
Like a skein of silk. [*Exit* BOSOLA.]

[*Enter* Cardinal, *followed by* Servants.]

*Card.* Where are you?
*Julia.* Here.
*Card.* Let none upon your lives
Have conference with the Prince Ferdinand,
Unless I know it: [*Exeunt* Servants.]
—[*Aside*] in this distraction
He may reveal the murder.
Yon's my ling'ring consumption:

***207–8. like the mice...houses:*** Cf. Rats desert a sinking ship. ***212. calling:*** profession. ***221. seal'd:*** fulfilled. ***228. ling'ring consumption:*** He is weary of her and wants to get rid of her, but she clings to him like a lingering disease.

I am weary of her; and by any means
Would be quit of.
*Julia.* How now, my lord?
What ails you?
*Card.* Nothing.
*Julia.* O, you are much alter'd:
Come, I must be your secretary, and remove
This lead from off your bosom—what's the matter?
*Card.* I may not tell you.
*Julia.* Are you so far in love with sorrow,
You cannot part with part of it? or think you
I cannot love your grace when you are sad,
As well as merry? or do you suspect
I, that have been a secret to your heart
These many winters, cannot be the same
Unto your tongue?
*Card.* Satisfy thy longing—
The only way to make thee keep my counsel
Is not to tell thee.
*Julia.* Tell your echo this,
Or flatterers that like echoes still report
What they hear though most imperfect, and not me:
For, if that you be true unto yourself,
I'll know.
*Card.* Will you rack me?
*Julia.* No, judgement shall
Draw it from you: it is an equal fault
To tell one's secrets unto all, or none.
*Card.* The first argues folly.
*Julia.* But the last tyranny.
*Card.* Very well—why imagine I have committed
Some secret deed, which I desire the world
May never hear of.
*Julia.* Therefore may not I know it?
You have conceal'd for me as great a sin
As adultery:—sir, never was occasion
For perfect trial of my constancy

***232. a secretary:*** a person in whom you can confide.

Till now: sir, I beseech you.

*Card.* You'll repent it.

*Julia.* Never.

*Card.* It hurries thee to ruin: I'll not tell thee—
Be well advis'd, and think what danger 'tis
To receive a prince's secrets: they that do,
Had need have their breasts hoop'd with adamant
To contain them: I pray thee yet be satisfy'd;
Examine thine own frailty; 'tis more easy
To tie knots, than unloose them:—'tis a secret
That, like a ling'ring poison, may chance lie
Spread in thy veins, and kill thee seven year hence.

*Julia.* Now you dally with me.

*Card.* No more; thou shalt know it.
By my appointment, the great Duchess of Malfi,
And two of her young children, four nights since,
Were strangled.

*Julia.* O heaven! sir, what have you done?

*Card.* How now? How settles this? Think you your bosom
Will be a grave, dark and obscure enough,
For such a secret?

*Julia.* You have undone yourself, sir.

*Card.* Why?

*Julia.* It lies not in me to conceal it.

*Card.* No?
Come, I will swear you to't upon this book.

*Julia.* Most religiously.

*Card.* Kiss it. [*She kisses the book.*]
Now you shall never utter it; thy curiosity
Hath undone thee: thou'rt poison'd with that book;
Because I knew thou couldst not keep my counsel,
I have bound thee to't by death.

[*Enter* BOSOLA.]

*Bos.* For pity-sake, hold!

*Card.* Ha, Bosola!

***263–4. frailty…unloose them:*** A woman's proverbial frailty that she cannot keep secrets. It will get her into trouble, if not now, then later. ***274. It lies not…it:*** because Bosola is hidden and has overheard everything. See l. 284.

*Julia.* I forgive you—
This equal piece of justice you have done,
For I betray'd your counsel to that fellow:
He overheard it; that was the cause I said
It lay not in me to conceal it.
*Bos.* O foolish woman,
Couldst not thou have poison'd him?
*Julia.* 'Tis weakness,
Too much to think what should have been done—I go,
I know not whither. [*Dies.*]
*Card.* Wherefore com'st thou hither?
*Bos.* That I might find a great man, like yourself,
Not out of his wits as the Lord Ferdinand,
To remember my service.
*Card.* I'll have thee hew'd in pieces.
*Bos.* Make not yourself such a promise of that life
Which is not yours to dispose of.
*Card.* Who plac'd thee here?
*Bos.* Her lust, as she intended.
*Card.* Very well,
Now you know me for your fellow murderer.
*Bos.* And wherefore should you lay fair marble colours
Upon your rotten purposes to me?
Unless you imitate some that do plot great treasons,
And when they have done, go hide themselves i'th' graves
Of those were actors in't?
*Card.* No more, there is a fortune attends thee.
*Bos.* Shall I go sue to Fortune any longer?
'Tis the fool's pilgrimage.
*Card.* I have honours in store for thee.
*Bos.* There are a many ways that conduct to seeming
Honour, and some of them very dirty ones.
*Card.* Throw to the devil
Thy melancholy: the fire burns well,
What need we keep a stirring of 't, and make
A greater smother? thou wilt kill Antonio?

***297–8. fair marble...purposes:*** paint over rotten wood so that it resembles marble. Hide your evil.

*Bos.* Yes.
*Card.* Take up that body.
*Bos.* I think I shall
Shortly grow the common bier for churchyards.
*Card.* I will allow thee some dozen of attendants
To aid thee in the murder.
*Bos.* O, by no means:

Physicians that apply horse-leeches to any rank swelling use to cut off their tails, that the blood may run through them the faster; let me have no train when I go to shed blood, lest it make me have a greater when I ride to the gallows.

*Card.* Come to me after midnight, to help to remove that body to her own lodging: I'll give out she died o'th plague; 'twill breed the less inquiry after her death.

*Bos.* Where's Castruchio, her husband?
*Card.* He's rode to Naples to take possession
Of Antonio's citadel.
*Bos.* Believe me, you have done a very happy turn.
*Card.* Fail not to come:—there is the master-key
Of our lodgings; and by that you may conceive
What trust I plant in you.
*Bos.* You shall find me ready.

*Exit* Cardinal.

O poor Antonio, though nothing be so needful
To thy estate as pity, yet I find
Nothing so dangerous. I must look to my footing:
In such slippery ice-pavements, men had need
To be frost-nail'd well; they may break their necks else.
The precedent's here afore me: how this man
Bears up in blood! seems fearless! Why, 'tis well:
Security some men call the suburbs of hell,
Only a dead wall between. Well, good Antonio,

***330–4. O poor Antonio…well:*** I cannot afford to feel pity for you, I must protect myself first. ***334. frost-nailed:*** hob-nailed shoes to prevent slipping upon ice. ***337. security:*** The word then had also the unfavourable sense of 'much' vain confidence (cf. *Macbeth* (III. v. 32–3). ***338–49. Well, good Antonio…them up:*** Bosola seems repentant enough here, but how genuine he is, is debatable. It is not until Sc. iv. 31, when he overhears that the Cardinal plans to murder him, and when he is convinced that he will get nothing that he finally turns against the Cardinal.

I'll seek thee out, and all my care shall be
To put thee into safety from the reach
Of these most cruel biters, that have got
Some of thy blood already. It may be
I'll join with thee, in a most just revenge.
The weakest arm is strong enough, that strikes
With the sword of justice:—still methinks the duchess
Haunts me: there, there!—
'Tis nothing but my melancholy.
O Penitence, let me truly taste thy cup,
That throws men down, only to raise them up. *Exit.*

*342. **thy blood:*** thy family, i.e. Antonio's children.

## Scene iii

*Enter* ANTONIO *and* DELIO.
[*There is an*] ECHO *from the* Duchess' *grave.*

*Delio.* Yon's the cardinal's window:—this fortification
Grew from the ruins of an ancient abbey;
And to yon side o'th' river, lies a wall,
Piece of a cloister, which in my opinion
Gives the best echo that you ever heard,
So hollow, and so dismal, and withal
So plain in the distinction of our words,
That many have suppos'd it is a spirit
That answers.

*Ant.* I do love these ancient ruins:
We never tread upon them but we set
Our foot upon some reverend history.
And questionless, here in this open court,
Which now lies naked to the injuries
Of stormy weather, some men lie interr'd
Lov'd the church so well, and gave so largely to't,
They thought it should have canopy'd their bones
Till doomsday; but all things have their end:
Churches and cities, which have diseases like to men,
Must have like death that we have.

*Echo.* *Like death that we have.*

*Delio.* Now the echo hath caught you:—

This lyrical scene is Webster's invention. It does not exist in Painter but the idea is not entirely an innovation on the part of Webster, because the echo-scene device is a stage tradition occurring in Lodge's *The Wounds of Civil War,* Wilson's *Cobbler's Prophecy* (printed 1594), Dekker's *Old Fortunatus,* Taylor's *The Hog Has Lost His Pearl* and Jonson's *Cynthia's Revels*. There is also a well-known echo scene in Guarini in the Italian tragi-comedy *Il Pastor Fido* available in English, and in English translation since 1602. There is a suggestion that the echo is not merely a sound-effect but, coming as it is from the Duchess's grave, a hallucinatory appearance of the Duchess's ghost. At one point, Antonio imagines that he sees the Duchess's face (42–5). All this heightens the atmosphere of the scene. The words that are echoed back are prophetic and very suggestive: 'Deadly accent', 'a thing of sorrow', 'Do not', 'Be mindful of your safety', 'O fly your fate', 'Thou art a dead thing'. ***12. questionless:*** undoubtedly.

*Ant.* It groan'd methought, and gave
A very deadly accent.
*Echo.* *Deadly accent.*
*Delio.* I told you 'twas a pretty one: you may make it
A huntsman, or a falconer, a musician,
Or a thing of sorrow.
*Echo.* *A thing of sorrow.*
*Delio.* Ay sure: that suits it best.
*Echo.* *That suits it best.*
*Delio.* 'Tis very like my wife's voice.
*Echo.* *Ay, wife's voice.*
*Delio .* Come, let's walk farther from't:—
I would not have you go to th' cardinal's tonight:
Do not.
*Echo.* *Do not.*
*Delio.* Wisdom doth not more moderate wasting sorrow
Than time: take time for't; be mindful of thy safety.
*Echo.* *Be mindful of thy safety.*
*Ant.* Necessity compels me:
Make scrutiny throughout the passes
Of your own life, you'll find it impossible
To fly your fate.
*Echo.* *O, fly your fate!*
*Delio.* Hark: the dead stones seem to have pity on you
And give you good counsel.
*Ant.* Echo, I will not talk with thee,
For thou art a dead thing.
*Echo.* *Thou art a dead thing.*
*Ant.* My duchess is asleep now,
And her little ones, I hope sweetly: O heaven,
Shall I never see her more?
*Echo.* *Never see her more.*
*Ant.* I mark'd not one repetition of the echo
But that: and on the sudden, a clear light
Presented me a face folded in sorrow.
*Delio.* Your fancy, merely.
*Ant.* Come: I'll be out of this ague;
For to live thus is not indeed to live:
It is a mockery, and abuse of life—
I will not henceforth save myself by halves;

Lose all, or nothing.
*Delio.* Your own virtue save you!
I'll fetch your eldest son, and second you;
It may be that the sight of his own blood
Spread in so sweet a figure may beget
The more compassion.
*Ant.* How ever, fare you well:
Though in our miseries Fortune have a part,
Yet in our noble suff'rings she hath none—
Contempt of pain, that we may call our own. *Exeunt.*

***53. his own blood:*** the Cardinal's. Antonio's son is the Duchess's son and therefore related by blood to the Cardinal.

## Scene iv

*Enter* Cardinal, PESCARA, MALATESTE, RODERIGO, *and* GRISOLAN.

*Card.* You shall not watch tonight by the sick prince,
His grace is very well recover'd.
*Mal.* Good my lord, suffer us.
*Card.* O, by no means;
The noise, and change of object in his eye,
Doth more distract him: I pray, all to bed,
And though you hear him in his violent fit,
Do not rise, I entreat you.
*Pes.* So sir, we shall not—
*Card.* Nay, I must have you promise
Upon your honours, for I was enjoin'd to't
By himself; and he seem'd to urge it sensibly.
*Pes.* Let our honours bind this trifle.
*Card.* Nor any of your followers.
*Mal.* Neither.
*Card.* It may be to make trial of your promise
When he's asleep, myself will rise, and feign
Some of his mad tricks, and cry out for help,
And feign myself in danger.
*Mal.* If your throat were cutting,
I'd not come at you, now I have protested against it.
*Card.* Why, I thank you. [*Withdraws.*]
*Gris.* 'Twas a foul storm tonight.
*Rod.* The Lord Ferdinand's chamber shook like an osier.
*Mal.* 'Twas nothing but pure kindness in the devil
To rock his own child. *Exeunt* [*all except the* Cardinal].
*Card.* The reason why I would not suffer these
About my brother, is because at midnight
I may with better privacy convey

***13–16. It may be...danger:*** Ironically, the Cardinal thus seals his own doom and when he is in real, not feigned danger, no one comes to help him. ***19. osier:*** a willow tree, not a reed.

Julia's body to her own lodging:—
O, my conscience!
I would pray now: but the devil takes away my heart
For having any confidence in prayer.
About this hour I appointed Bosola
To fetch the body: when he hath serv'd my turn,
He dies. *Exit.*

*Enter* BOSOLA.

*Bos.* Hah? 'twas the cardinal's voice: I heard him name
Bosola, and my death: listen, I hear one's footing.

*Enter* FERDINAND.

*Ferd.* Strangling is a very quiet death.
*Bos.[Aside]* Nay then, I see I must stand upon my guard.
*Ferd.* What say' to that? whisper, softly: do you agree to't?
So it must be done i'th' dark: the cardinal
Would not for a thousand pounds the doctor should
see it. *Exit.*
*Bos.* My death is plotted; here's the consequence of murder:
*We value not desert, nor Christian breath,*
*When we know black deeds must be cur'd with death.*

*Enter* ANTONIO *and* Servant.

*Serv.* Here stay sir, and be confident, I pray:
I'll fetch you a dark lantern. *Exit.*
*Ant.* Could I take him at his prayers,
There were hope of pardon.
*Bos.* Fall right my sword! [*Stabs him.*]
I'll not give thee so much leisure as to pray.
*Ant.* O, I am gone! Thou hast ended a long suit
In a minute.
*Bos.* What art thou?
*Ant.* A most wretched thing,
That only have thy benefit in death,
To appear myself.

*26. O, my conscience:* Even as he talks of conscience, he is planning Bosola's death (l. 3).

[*Enter* Servant *with a light.*]

*Serv.* Where are you, sir?
*Ant.* Very near my home:—Bosola!
*Ant.* O, misfortune!
*Bos.* Smother thy pity, thou art dead else:—Antonio!
The man I would have sav'd 'bove mine own life!
We are merely the stars' tennis-balls, struck and banded
Which way please them—O good Antonio,
I'll whisper one thing in thy dying ear
Shall make thy heart break quickly: Thy fair duchess
And two sweet children—
*Ant.* Their very names
Kindle a little life in me.
*Bos.* Are murder'd!
*Ant.* Some men have wish'd to die
At the hearing of sad tidings: I am glad
That I shall do't in sadness; I would not now
Wish my wounds balm'd, nor heal'd, for I have no use
To put my life to. In all our quest of greatness,
Like wanton boys whose pastime is their care,
We follow after bubbles, blown in th' air.
Pleasure of life, what is't? only the good hours
Of an ague; merely a preparative to rest,
To endure vexation:— I do not ask
The process of my death; only commend me
To Delio.
*Bos.* Break heart!—
*Ant.* And let my son fly the courts of princes.[*Dies.*]
*Bos.* Thou seem'st to have lov'd Antonio?
*Serv.* I brought him hither,
To have reconcil'd him to the cardinal.
*Bos.* I do not ask thee that:—
Take him up, if thou tender thine own life,
And bear him, where the Lady Julia
Was wont to lodge.—O, my fate moves swift!

***62. in sadness:*** (1) in sorrow (2) in earnest. ***65. Like wanton boys:*** Compare Cardinal Wolsey's speech in *Henry VIII* (III.ii.358–60): 'I have ventur'd/ Like little wanton boys that swim on bladders/ This many a summer in a sea of glory.'

I have this cardinal in the forge already,
Now I'll bring him to th' hammer:—O direful misprision!
I will not imitate things glorious,
No more than base: I'll be mine own example.
On, on: and look thou represent, for silence,
The thing thou bear'st. *Exeunt.*

***80. misprision:*** mistake.

## Scene v

*Enter* Cardinal, *with a book.*

*Card.* I am puzzled in a question about hell:
He says, in hell there's one material fire,
And yet it shall not burn all men alike.
Lay him by:—how tedious is a guilty conscience!
When I look into the fish-ponds, in my garden,
Methinks I see a thing, arm'd with a rake
That seems to strike at me:—

*Enter* BOSOLA, *and* Servant *with* ANTONIO'S *body.*

Now! art thou come?
Thou look'st ghastly:
There sits in thy face some great determination,
Mix'd with some fear.

*Bos.* Thus it lightens into action:
I am come to kill thee.

*Card.* Hah? help! our guard!

*Bos.* Thou art deceiv'd:
They are out of thy howling.

*Card.* Hold: and I will faithfully divide
Revenues with thee.

*Bos.* Thy prayers and proffers
Are both unseasonable.

*Card.* Raise the watch!
We are betray'd!

*Bos.* I have confin'd your flight:
I'll suffer your retreat to Julia's chamber
But no further.

*Card.* Help! we are betray'd!

*Enter* [, *above*,] PESCARA, MALATESTE, RODERIGO
[, *and* GRISOLAN].

**Stage directions.** ***with a book:*** often a stage device for soliloquies. ***6. a thing...rake:*** i.e. the devil. ***10. it lightens...action:*** moves rapidly into action.

*Mal.* Listen: —
*Card.* My dukedom for rescue!
*Rod.* Fie upon his counterfeiting!
*Mal.* Why, 'tis not the cardinal.
*Rod.* Yes, yes, 'tis he:
But I'll see him hang'd, ere I'll go down to him.
*Card.* Here's a plot upon me, I am assaulted! I am lost,
Unless some rescue!
*Gris.* He doth this pretty well:
But it will not serve to laugh me out of mine honour.
*Card.* The sword's at my throat:—
*Rod.* You would not bawl so loud then.
*Mal.* Come, come:
Let's go to bed: he told us thus much aforehand.
*Pes.* He wish'd you should not come at him: but believe't,
The accent of the voice sounds not in jest.
I'll down to him, howsoever, and with engines
Force ope the doors. [*Exit above.*]
*Rod.* Let's follow him aloof,
And note how the cardinal will laugh at him.

[*Exeunt, above,* MALATESTE, RODERIGO, *and* GRISOLAN.]

*Bos.* There's for you first— *He kills the servant.*
'Cause you shall not unbarricade the door
To let in rescue.
*Card.* What cause hast thou to pursue my life?
*Bos.* Look there:—
*Card.* Antonio!
*Bos.* Slain by my hand unwittingly: —
Pray, and be sudden; when thou kill'd'st thy sister,
Thou took'st from Justice her most equal balance,
And left her naught but her sword.
*Card.* O, mercy!
*Bos.* Now it seems thy greatness was only outward;
For thou fall'st faster of thyself, than calamity
Can drive thee. I'll not waste longer time: there!
[*Stabs him.*]
*Card.* Thou hast hurt me:—
*Bos.* Again! [*Stabs him again.*]

*Card.* Shall I die like a leveret
Without any resistance? help, help, help!
I am slain!

*Enter* FERDINAND.

*Ferd.* Th' alarum! give me a fresh horse:
Rally the vaunt-guard, or the day is lost:
Yield, yield! I give you the honour of arms,
Shake my sword over you—will you yield?

*Card.* Help me, I am your brother.

*Ferd.* The devil!
My brother fight upon the adverse party?
There flies your ransom. *He wounds the Cardinal, and in the scuffle gives Bosola his death-wound.*

*Card.* O Justice!
I suffer now, for what hath former been:
*Sorrow is held the eldest child of sin.*

*Ferd.* Now you're brave fellows:—Caesar's fortune was harder than Pompey's; Caesar died in the arms of prosperity, Pompey at the feet of disgrace:—you both died in the field. The pain's nothing: pain many times is taken away with the apprehension of greater, as the toothache with the sight of a barber that comes to pull it out—there's philosophy for you.

*Bos.* Now my revenge is perfect: *He kills Ferdinand.*
sink, thou main cause
Of my undoing!—The last part of my life
Hath done me best service.

*Ferd.* Give me some wet hay, I am broken-winded—
I do account this world but a dog-kennel:
I will vault credit, and affect high pleasures,
Beyond death.

***45. leveret:*** small hare. ***48. vaunt-guard:*** the advance party of an army. ***56–8. Caesar's ...disgrace:*** taken from Whetstone, *Heptameron* (1582): 'What difference was there between the Fortunes of Caesar and Pompey, when their endes were both violent: save that I hould Caesars to be the harder: for that he was murthered in the Armes of Prosperytie and Pompey, at the feet of Disgrace'. ***66. broken-winded:*** Ferdinand imagines that he is a horse that is out of breath. ***68. vault:*** overleap.

*Bos.* He seems to come to himself,
Now he's so near the bottom.
*Ferd.* My sister! O! my sister! There's the cause on't:
*Whether we fall by ambition, blood, or lust,*
*Like diamonds, we are cut with our own dust.* [*Dies.*]
*Card.* Thou hast thy payment too.
*Bos.* Yes, I hold my weary soul in my teeth,
'Tis ready to part from me:—I do glory
That thou, which stood'st like a huge pyramid
Begun upon a large and ample base,
Shalt end in a little point, a kind of nothing.

[*Enter* PESCARA, MALATESTE, RODERGO, *and* GRISOLAN.]

*Pes.* How now, my lord?
*Mal.* O, sad disaster!
*Rod.* How comes this?
*Bos.* Revenge, for the Duchess of Malfi, murdered
By th' Arragonian brethren; for Antonio,
Slain by this hand; for lustful Julia,
Poison'd by this man; and lastly, for myself,
That was an actor in the main of all
Much 'gainst mine own good nature, yet i'th' end
Neglected.
*Pes.* How now, my lord?
*Card.* Look to my brother:
He gave us these large wounds, as we were struggling
Here i'th' rushes:— and now, I pray, let me
Be laid by, and never thought of. [*Dies.*]
*Pes.* How fatally, it seems, he did withstand
His own rescue.
*Mal.* Thou wretched thing of blood,
How came Antonio by his death?
*Bos.* In a mist: I know not how—
Such a mistake as I have often seen
In a play:—O, I am gone!—
We are only like dead walls, or vaulted graves,
That ruin'd, yields no echo:—Fare you well—

***85. an actor...all:*** See Introduction p. xl. ***92. thing of blood:*** instrument of death.
***98. yields no echo:*** contrast the echoing wall in V.iii.

It may be pain, but no harm to me to die
In so good a quarrel. O, this gloomy world!
In what a shadow, or deep pit of darkness,
Doth womanish and fearful mankind live!
Let worthy minds ne'er stagger in distrust
To suffer death, or shame for what is just—
Mine is another voyage. [*Dies.*]

*Pes.* The noble Delio, as I came to th' palace,
Told me of Antonio's being here, and show'd me
A pretty gentleman, his son and heir.

*Enter* DELIO [*with* Antonio's Son].

*Mal.* O sir, you come too late!

*Delio.* I heard so, and
Was arm'd for't ere I came. Let us make noble use
Of this great ruin; and join all our force
To establish this young, hopeful gentleman
In's mother's right. These wretched eminent things
Leave no more fame behind 'em than should one
Fall in a frost, and leave his print in snow;
As soon as the sun shines, it ever melts,
Both form, and matter:— I have ever thought
Nature doth nothing so great, for great men,
As when she's pleas'd to make them lords of truth:
*Integrity of life is fame's best friend,*
*Which nobly, beyond death, shall crown the end.*

*Exeunt.*

# Suggestions for Further Reading

### *A. Editions*

The complete works of John Webster are available in the edition by F.L. Lucas (4 vols.), London, 1927. A more handy edition of selected plays of Webster is *Three Plays: The White Devil, The Duchess of Malfi, The Devil's Law Case* (Middlesex, Penguin Books, 1985) with a useful introduction by D.C. Gunby. There is a separate edition of *The Duchess of Malfi* by Frederick Alleyn (London, 1963) but the most reliable edition is in the Revels Plays Series (Methuen, London,1964), edited by John Russel Brown. In the same series J. R. Brown has also edited *The White Devil.* These two great tragedies of Webster are closely related to each other and it is advisable to read *The White Devil* for a closer understanding of *The Duchess of Malfi.* Elizabeth Brennan's editions of the plays in Ernest Benn's New Mermaid Series are also good and handy editions.

The student should be familiar with some of the major Jacobean tragedies: John Marston's *The Malcontent,* George Chapman's *Bussy d'Ambois* and *The Revenge of Bussy d'Ambois,* Cyril Tourneur's *The Revenger's Tragedy* and *The Atheist's Tragedy,* John Ford's *'Tis Pity She's a Whore* and Thomas Middleton's *The Changeling.* As Kyd's *The Spanish Tragedy*, though written much earlier, is the first significant play written in the Revenge Tragedy tradition, this play should also be included in the reading list.

For the background of the age it is best to begin with the two essays by L.G. Salingar, 'The Social Setting' and 'The Elizabethan Literary Renaissance' in *A Guide to English Literature*, edited by Boris Ford, vol. II (Middlesex, Penguin, 1982). E.M.W. Tillyard discusses the transition from medieval to Renaissance modes of thought in *The Elizabethan World Picture* (London, 1960) while L.C. Knights analyses the social and economic background in *Drama and Society in the Age of Jonson* (London, 1937).

## *B. Criticism*

Many critical works have been written on John Webster and the drama of his age, but as interpretations vary from critic to critic, the student is advised to become familiar with the text of the play first, before proceeding to the conflicting critical opinions.

The following books are suggested for further reading.

**John Webster: Select Reading List**

Bradbrook, M.C. *John Webster, Citizen and Dramatist*. London: Weidenfeld and Nicolson, 1980.

Brooke, Rupert. *John Webster and the Elizabethan Drama*. London: Sidwick and Jackson, 1916.

Forker, C.R. *The Skull Beneath the Skin: The Achievement of John Webster.* Carbondale and Edwardsville: Southern Illinois University Press, 1986.

Holdsworth, R.V., ed. *Webster, 'The White Devil', and 'The Duchess of Malfi'*. London: Macmillan, 6th Impression, 1993.

Hunter, G.K. and S.K., ed. *John Webster: A Critical Anthology.* Middlesex: Penguin, 1969.

Leech, Clifford. *John Webster: The Duchess of Malfi. Studies in English Literature*, S. No. 8. London: Edward Arnold, 1963.

Morris, Brian, ed. *John Webster, Mermaid Critical Commentaries.* London: Ernest Benn, 1972 (1970).

Pearson, Jaquelin. *Tragedy and Tragicomedy in the Plays of John Webster*. Manchester: Manchester University Press, 1980.

Price, Hereward, T. 'The Function of Imagery in Webster', *PMLA*, 70 (1955). Also included in Ralph Kaufman, *Elizabethan Drama, Modern Essays in Criticism.* New York: OUP, 1961, rpt., Routledge, 1991.

Rabkin, Norman. *Twentieth Century Interpretations of* The Duchess of Malfi*: A Collection of Critical Essays.* New Jersey: Prentice Hall, 1968.

**Other Dramatists**

John Marston, *The Changeling*

Thomas Middleton, *The Malcontent*

George Chapman, *Bussy d' Ambois, Revenge of Bussy d'Ambois*

Cyril Tourneur, *The Revenger's Tragedy, The Atheist's Tragedy*

John Ford, *'Tis Pity She's a Whore*

Thomas Kyd, *The Spanish Tragedy*

**Editions**

*Complete Works* (Four Volumes). Ed. F.L.Lucas. London: Chatto and Windus, 1927.

*Three Plays: 'The White Devil', 'The Duchess of Malfi', ' The Devil's Law Case'*. Ed. D.C. Gunby. Middlesex: Penguin, 1985.

*The Duchess of Malfi* (Revels Plays). Ed. John Russel Brown. London: Methuen, 1964.

*The Duchess of Malfi.* Ed. Elizabeth Brennan in Ernest Brennan's Third New Mermaid Edition. London: A&C Black (Publishers) Ltd., 1993.

*The White Devil* (Revels Plays). Ed. John Russel Brown. Manchester: Manchester University Press, 1960.

**Background of the Age**

Knights, L.C. *Drama and Society in the Age of Jonson.* London: Chatto and Windus, 1937.

Salinger, L.G. 'The Social Setting' and 'The Elizabethan Literary Renascence' in *A Guide to English Literature*, Volume II. Ed. Boris Ford. Middlesex: Penguin, 1982.

Tillyard, E.M.W. *The Elizabethan World Picture.* New York: Random House, 1959.

**Elizabethan and Jacobean Drama**

Bowers, F. *Elizabethan Revenge Tragedy, 1587–1642.* Princeton: Princeton University Press, 1940, rpt. 1970.

Bradbrook, M.C. *Themes and Conventions of Elizabethan Tragedy*. Cambridge: Cambridge University Press, 1957.

Ellis-Fermor, Una. *Jacobean Drama*. London: Methuen, 1936.

Kaufman, Ralph. *Elizabethan Drama, Modern Essays in Criticism*. New York: OUP, 1961, rpt. Routledge, 1991.

Ribner, Irving. *Jacobean Tragedy: The Quest for Moral Disorder*. London: Methuen, 1979.

Simpson, P. 'The Theme of Revenge in Elizabethan Tragedy' (Proceedings of the British Academy XXI), *British Academy Shakespeare Lectures*. Oxford: Oxford University Press, 1936.

Tomlinson, T.B. *A Study of Elizabethan and Jacobean Tragedy*. Cambridge: Cambridge University Press, 1964.

Wilson, F.P. *Elizabethan and Jacobean*. Oxford: Clarendon Press, 1945.

# Topics for Discussion

1. The influence of Seneca and Machiavelli on *The Duchess of Malfi.*
2. The theme of madness in *The Duchess of Malfi.*
3. Contrasts in evil: analysis of the characters of the Cardinal, Ferdinand and Bosola.
4. The significance of iterative images in *The Duchess of Malfi.*
5. Religious symbolism in *The Duchess of Malfi.*
6. Account for the gloom that pervades Jacobean tragedy with special reference to *The Duchess of Malfi.*
7. Is *The Duchess of Malfi* a revenge play?
8. Would you describe *The Duchess of Malfi* as 'decadent drama'?
9. The patriarchal setting in *The Duchess of Malfi.*
10. Does *The Duchess of Malfi* conclude with a sense of negation and despair?
11. Webster is superb in building up atmosphere but is weak in plot construction. Do you agree?
12. Analyse the character of *The Duchess of Malfi* as the type of emergent woman power.
13. What is the significance of the changes that Webster has made to his source material?